END OF MY RAINBOW

Sholabomi Joseph

ISBN: 1507823045
ISBN 13: 9781507823040
Library of Congress Control Number: 2015902499
CreateSpace Independent Publishing Platform
North Charleston, South Carolina

To my wonderful children for believing in me

CHAPTER ONE

'Good morning, Mama', I say, stretching slowly with a long, drawn-out yawn.

'Good morning, my child. Did you sleep well?' 'Yes, Mama, I did'.

I am growing up with Mama in humble accommodations—well, I was brought to live with Mama, as I am often reminded during times of adolescent rebellion. Not that I am a rebellious child, but once in a while, I exercise my right of rebellion as a child. Mama and I live in the newly developing area of Obalande, where bungalows appear to have emerged from the marshland. They are all different colours but have pretty much the same structure and sit next to a newly tarred road that seems to melt in the hot, sunny mirage of the afternoon. That street has become my playground, where friendships have been made, friendships broken. Mama loves me with all the love a mother gives her child. She is actually my Paternal grandmother, but I know no other love but that of Mama.

Also living in the bungalow is J. Kurumbah. J. Kurumbah! Kurumbah! I hear his friend, Mr Doregos, call his name from the front door, so I guess that's his name. We don't see much of J. Kurumbah; he leaves quite early in the morning and comes back late at night. J. Kurumbah never says much to Mama, says nothing to me. All I notice is that whenever J. Kurumbah is approaching, Mama will whisk me away from his sight into the safety of her bedroom, as if hiding me from some impending danger.

I don't remember much from that early age, except that I have a super sixth sense of hypnotherapy to go way back in time to pre-Obalende years—not that it makes any difference, but it's good to know. I do remember, however, how Mama walked me to The Young Shall Grow nursery school. It was quite a long walk from home, but every bit of the journey was an adventure—and an enjoyable one, too, in the company of Mama. I remember her carrying me halfway when my little legs tired from the hot afternoon sun and buying me Penguin ice cream to quench my thirst.

'Tolani, come turn the handle of the sewing machine', Mama tells me one day. 'You must learn how to sew and become a good seamstress like me'.

'Yes, Mama. I want to sew like you'.

As I turn the handle of the Singer sewing machine, the whrr, whrr, whrr sound is like a gentle lullaby that causes me to doze off.

When not learning how to sew, I play with Tunde, who lives in the next bungalow. Tunde is much older than me, always in khaki shorts and danshiki tops. He has gangly legs and wears brown sandals. Sometimes Tunde exhibits some strange behaviour for a boy, but this makes me crack up, laugh, and roll on the warm sand in the backyard. Tunde pretends he is a pregnant woman, stuffing clothes up his danshiki top and waddling like a pregnant woman.

'Tolani! Tolani!' Mama calls from the kitchen window, having seen Tunde playing his strange game. 'Come in right now!' she orders. 'I must never see you play with that strange boy ever again'.

'But why not, Mama?'

'Child, don't ask questions', she says, wagging her finger at me. I know not to ask any further questions, and from the corner of my eye, I see Tunde slowly making his way into his house. Tunde has an older brother, Ade. Ade is not always around because he lives in a boarding house. But his presence is known when he comes back for the holidays. He belts out James Brown from the gramophone, and I enjoy learning the lyrics. My favourite is 'Say it loud, am black and proud', or the one Mama forbids me to sing: 'Get up, ah! Get on it! Sex machine, get on it!'

Soon after that, Tunde stops coming out to play in the backyard, and I guess this is the end of our backyard friendship.

I busy myself by learning more sewing skills on the Singer machine. I have gotten used to being in my own company, playing on the veranda when Mama takes an afternoon nap. On this fateful hot and sunny afternoon, my journey of questions will start. I hear J. Kurumbah approaching—I know from his slow footsteps. He gets closer to the open space of the veranda and takes sight of me, still sitting there, unmoved by his presence.

'Woman, woman! I told you to take this bastard child back to where she belongs. Take her back to her house girl, Mother', he shouts angrily to Mama.

I feel a hand grab me from behind. Mama wakes up and pulls me inside the room, quickly shuts the door, and tries hard to keep me from hearing J. Kurumbah. For some reason, I awoke some anger in J. Kurumbah. From that day, Mama makes sure that incident never happens again.

But I need to know why. I will sneak to Tunde's house and ask questions. He will know; he is much older than me. No, that's not a good Idea. I will wait out on the streets, and I am sure he will come and join me and the other children playing on the street. Then I will ask him.

Mama is a God-fearing, good Christian and never misses Sunday church or Friday prayer meetings. Sunday-morning preparation for church is a ritual in itself, as the stretching comb heats over the coal-pot fire. I keep still so my ears won't get singed as Mama combs out my tangled Afro puff into smooth, straight hair that is neatly tied into ribbons, ready for church. I enjoy all the attention at church from Mama's friends and the Sunday School master. I enjoy a treat of cabin biscuits as the most well behaved in Sunday School for reciting the Lord's Prayer by heart.

The morning ritual of hair stretching has changed. Now Aunty puts my hair in braids. Aunty visits every Saturday, braids my hair, and stays 'til quite late in the evening. On every visit, she brings treats that are even better than cabin biscuits—English apples, juicy red, and green English apples. Yes, Nigeria, being post-Colonial, is still enjoying imports. I am beginning to become attached to this newfound friendship and warmth and look forward to Saturdays, but not when it's time for her departure. I throw tantrums and upset myself and everyone around me. It really breaks me to have to wait for a whole week before seeing Aunty again. I want to go with Aunty and eat more treats and juicy apples.

After my Saturday episode of tantrums, I notice that Aunty's visits become less frequent and farther between, until they stop altogether. Mama stopped the hair stretching, and my hair got back its kinky Afroness. I wonder, *Why won't Aunty visit anymore? Where has she gone?*

I am sitting on the veranda and watching the sun go down with Mama. I'm eating freshly boiled corn on the cob, and between mouthfuls, I ask, 'Mama, what is a "bastard child"?' She does not answer. So I ask, 'Is my mother really a house girl like Bintu

Without looking at me, Mama answers in her most stern voice, 'Child, you'd better shut your mouth and eat what you are eating, lest you choke'. But still, I wonder in my mind is my Mother Aunty? The fondness love and care, quietly I have a strong suspicion she is my Mother.

The rainy season is approaching, and it pours non-stop; it's called the 'seven days' rain'. During a brief lull in the spell, I sit on the veranda, listening to the echo of the fish hawker calling out, 'Come buy fresh fish! Buy your crab. Cook some soup…'. I walk to the edge of the house waiting to call the hawker in as Mama had asked me to. And coming down the road, I see the figure of Tunde, walking with an unfamiliar gait, swinging and sashaying his hips. It has been a while since I last saw Tunde after that episode in the backyard. This strange walk does not look elegant on Tunde, and in khaki shorts, he looks quite a spectacle. I run up to him and say, 'Hello, Tunde. Can I come and play at your house?' The question defies Mama's instructions.

Tunde gives me a blank look, and, as if I am not there, continues his swaying and sashaying of the hips and disappears down the side of their bungalow. The other children on the streets burst out into fits of laughter. To be honest, seeing a man walk that way is quite unusual and funny at the same time. I feel sad. I have lost a friend. No more Mummy and Daddy games. Actually, I do not really care much about this silly game but just need someone to tell me the meaning of 'bastard child'. Knowing the answer might tell me something about who my mother is.

CHAPTER TWO

War breaks out in Nigeria. The relative calmness of the quiet Obalende street is broken. Curfews are imposed, and children are no longer able to play in the streets. There are tales of children being kidnapped and conscripted into the army. Sunday church going is now limited, and Friday prayer meeting is cancelled.

Even J. Kurumbah stops going out that much, but Mama is sure I am away from his sight. Food is running out. I hear Mama tell our neighbours that, and we are having to survive on stew made from bitter leaf plucked from the backyard, water leaf growing wild in the waterlogged marshes, and catfish in the ponds by the creek.

'Mama, why is there a war, and are we all going to be killed?' I ask.

Mama tries to explain in the simplest terms for my age. 'My child, the Igbo people are trying to take over Nigeria, and the Hausa and Yoruba people are trying to prevent this from happening and are fighting the Igbo army. But we are not going to die. No one is going to die', she reassures me calmly. But the look in her eyes cannot hide the uncertainty or the fear in her voice. But I trust Mama. If she says we are not going to die, then we are not going to die. The Igbos are fighting with the rest of Nigeria. I think, *No wonder I no longer see Chineye and her family, Emeka, Adaeze, or even Akachuwku.* That accounts for all the Igbos living on the street; they have gone with their parents to fight the Biafran War (also known as the Nigerian Civil War, 6 July 1967 to 15 January 1970). These are good friends whom I may never ever see again because of this war.

Suddenly the stolen peace and calmness of the sunny afternoon are shattered. A loud crash from next door is followed by blood-curdling screaming and running. Mama grabs me, and we run outside. Everyone is in the street, running up and down. There is a sudden urgency just to run in any direction for shelter. From what we gather, an enemy plane has been shot down on its mission to bomb the army headquarters, which is a few minutes' walk from the bungalows. Debris from the plane has fallen through Aunty Caro's house, narrowly missing her as she slept on the bed. The older people are running to the neighbouring street to see the blown-out plane and whatever remains of the wreckage. This is really scary for everyone. I can see that Mama is no longer comforted by her own words, and she is worried for the future and where it will lead.

After what seems like years—well, thirty months—of civil war, normality slowly returns. We are able to resume schooling but have to be accompanied by one or two parents of the other children for safeguarding. I sit with Mama and listen the transistor radio to the announcement from the BBC World Service that the war has ended. Not much jubilation for Mama, just relief that the fighting is over. Our bungalow is safe, but we are saddened for lives that have been lost and for displaced families. She waits for news from family members about her nephew, Uncle Mutairu, who joined the Nigerian Army and has been at the war front. From what she has been told, he is back but badly injured and recuperating at the family house in town.

'Stop it, stop it!' Other children around me are shouting, and some are screaming. I am being pummelled, rolling around on the grass, and being fed grass by this older girl, Ngozi. Ngozi has singled me out for a beating on this day. She seems to pick randomly whom she will beat up at the end of school every day. I cannot fight back; I do not have the strength to take her on. After what seems like ages, I am eventually saved by Mama Puff Puff who sells fried dumpling snacks, she pulls her off me. 'Wetin she do? Wetin she do?' Mama Puff Puff asks the other girls what I had done wrong.

'She dey laff me, she laff me say I kno sabi book, OK, no vex, no vex my pickens, you kno see say you big pass am, oya all of you make yo na de go home' as Mama Puff Puff placates Ngozi from getting upset at me for making fun of her and sends us all on our way home.

Ngozi is in the same class as I am but is much older than most of the girls, which is not unusual. Many children who missed out on education due to the Nigerian Civil War are placed in a mixed-age and -ability class in an attempt to 'push' them through basic primary education. Ireti Primary School is one such local government school, nestled between the army barracks and Ikoyi Prison. Though it is quite a trek from home, it is the best Mama can afford for me, and I make the journey to school with other children on the street.

Saved by Mama Puff Puff the fried dumpling seller, I dust myself off and check that my uniform is not torn. I will have to explain to Mama that I was in a fight—well, beaten up by Ngozi. Knowing Mama, she will accompany me to school, and Ngozi will have to face her wrath. I shudder at the thought of that happening. You see, Ngozi is the daughter of a soldier. I hear tales that anyone crossing the path of a soldier is locked up in the barracks and never seen or heard of again! I go home and say nothing to Mama. I'm just happy to be safe, at least for today. I will have to face Ngozi again the next day because she is my desk partner.

I will tell you a bit about Ireti School. As you may have guessed, it's a local community school. The teachers have probably been scarred by the effects of the civil war, trying to impart knowledge upon children even more scarred by the war and bringing normality back to teaching. They try their best, but the teaching is fragmented. What I enjoy most is listening to BBC Education Service. I like listening to narratives, stories being told by the voice of a woman. The teacher asks questions after each narration to ensure that we are paying attention.

Math lessons put the fright in any young child's mind. They are always fraught with the threat of lashings with the cane if one mixes up the recitation of the times (multiplication) table. I always feel like calling out for Mama to come save me. I've had a few lashings of the whip from being lazy with the times table, but the likes of Ngozi are never far from the crack of the cane whip, which is the main reason for her temper.

Rrriiiiiiing! goes the school bell signalling the end of the school day, and indeed the end of the school term. I pack my books, make a dash for the door, and run as fast as my little body will carry me, out and away from Ngozi, at least for the next eight weeks.

The long holiday is not much. I just play in the hot sun on the street with the other children. We play hop-scotch, skip, and play ten-ten, a clappy, clappy game of elimination and catch.

'Tolani! Tolani!' Mama calls. 'Go and put on your slippers. We're going to the market'.

I like going to the market with Mama because I get treats of honeycomb sweet, a local sweet of different, attractive colours made by the Malam the Hausa traders.

'Give me two hens and one cock', Mama says to the woman, and she brings them out of the cane basket. Mama holds them up and examines them closely. 'I don't want this one. Give me that brown one'. I watch as Mama haggles for the best price. This art of haggling I learn from Mama and perfect as I grow older.

'Mama, what are we going to do with all these chickens? Are we going to have a big Sunday party?'

'Be patient, my child. Be patient', she says. 'Tolani, these chickens are for you. From now on, you have to look after them, take care of them, feed them'.

I am delighted with the responsibility. We put them in the coop that the carpenter had constructed.

My new responsibility as a chicken farmer means I don't miss Tunde much. I never tire of sitting in the backyard, away from anywhere near J. Kurumbah, feeding my chickens corn grain and watching them scratch at the earth and make delicate patterns in the sand. They seem to own the compound, moving from one end to the other. Soon my population of chickens grows, my hens lay eggs, chicks hatch, and it is a wonderful feeling to watch them grow from yellow fluffy balls. I am very proud of being a 'chicken farmer'.

Some days, in the backyard, I catch a glimpse of Tunde. He has grown taller. He is no longer in khaki shorts but in khaki trousers and ankara fabric shirt. He sometimes gives me a limp wave, and I stop to wonder how he now seems to have adopted a new way of walking—you know, an effeminate cat walk, a swishing of the hips, don't really why this new adopted manner of walking but how very strange, how strange. How we have grown apart and stopped being friends, and now it's even more strange how he sashays down the road.

I know when Ade is back from boarding school because music is blaring from their gramophone to the backyard. The one I like listening to is James Brown. I bob along to the tune of 'Say it loud, am black and proud, say it loud, am black and proud'. As I bob along to the music, I leave trails of grain for my chickens to follow. One, two, three, four...hang on, something's not right. Last time I counted, I had eight chickens. Yes, I know because I know them well enough to know something is not right. Yes, that's it! The green-speckled-feather cockerel is missing. I count again, and this time I am sure the green-speckled-feather cockerel is missing. 'Mama! Mama! Mama!' I scream.

She comes running to the backyard.

'Mama, one chicken is missing! The green-speck-led-feather cockerel is missing'.

I begin to get into a tearful mode, frightful that something bad has happened.

'Calm down, child. Let's go and look in front. Maybe it's gone next door'.

'No, Mama, I just opened up the cage now, and it is not among the other chickens'.

'Coooo, cooooo, coooo', we call out for the missing cockerel. We look under the pitanga bush; maybe it got trapped in the roots and died there. We look over Aunty Caro's fence, up the almond tree, and up the ca-shew nut tree, but the green-speckled-feather cockerel is nowhere to be found.

'This is strange, my child', Mama says. 'Something is not right'.

Mama decides that every evening, once the chickens have gone to roost, I will secure the cage with a padlock and do a head count. The locking up of the cage seems to work, and for the time being, my chickens are safe.

━━◆ ◆━━

Easter is coming up soon, and that weekend, Mama takes me to town to buy me a pair of shoes for church on Easter Sunday. I have outgrown the black patent shoes Aunty gave me on her last visit. Once we are in the Bata shoe shop, I feel like trying on all the shoes, even the ones with the funny high heels—'Chubby Checka' heels—not that I can balance in them.

'Mama, I like these', I say, pointing at a pair of shiny patent red shoes with shiny black heels.

'You mean the Dolly shoes?' asks the attendant lady waiting to serve us.

'Yes, those ones, the Dolly shoes'.

I try them on, and it is as if they have been made to fit me perfectly.

'Bring her one size bigger', Mama tells the attendant. She does, and I parade in front of the mirror. Already in my head, I am picturing the perfect dress to match and ribbons for my Afro.

'Thank you, Mama!' I say, throwing my arms around her and giving her a big hug.

Shock! Horror! The chicken cage has been broken into; the padlock is broken. I let the chickens out and start a head count the following morning. Two chickens are gone—stolen.

'Mama! Mama!' I shout from the backyard. 'Mama, someone has stolen two chickens!' There are now five, and I count again. Mama comes out, and I start crying. 'Mama, who is stealing our chickens?'

Mama cannot give me an answer. She is as puzzled as I am, and because we need to keep the chicken population up, we do not eat chicken on Easter

Sunday. Instead, Mama cooks goat stew, which is even tastier.

'Thief! Thief! Thief!' someone is shouting, and it wakes us up early one morning. Mama sits up with a jolt, too scared to go out to listen. The voice gets louder and louder and seems to be coming from the backyard. Mama looks at the wall clock; it is barely 6:00 a.m. Though already sunrise, she ties her wrapper over her nightgown and creeps out toward the backyard with me in tow.

'Thief! Thief! Thief!' J. Kurumbah is holding the scruff of a young boy's shirt, and the boy is trying hard to wriggle free. He is still holding in his hand one of my chickens, which is also squawking for freedom. We get nearer, and J. Kurumbah releases the young man but first lets us take a good look at his face. The boy makes a dash for freedom, dropping my chicken before Mama can get a hold of him, but I know the face of that young man. J. Kurumbah saves the day and walks away without saying a word.

'Mama, I know that boy', I say. 'I know where he lives, and I will show you'.

'Oya. Come, let's go. Come and show me his house'.

So I take Mama, barefoot, to the top of the road where Rufus lives. Yes, that's his name. I sometimes play with his younger sisters. Rufus is much, much older than us, so he just sits on the fence outside his house and smokes cigarettes. It takes a while for Rufus's mum to answer the door. She says, 'Good morning, Mama. Hope there is no problem this early morning'.

'Good morning, Mama Rufus'. Mama is trying to hide the anger in her voice. 'Your son, Rufus, was caught this morning stealing my chicken'.

Mama Rufus's face falls with disappointment as she begins to apologise to Mama. 'Please, Mama. I am sorry and will make sure it never happens again'.

It does not happen again because we do not see Rufus again, and our chickens are safe.

The rainy season comes, unrelenting with thunder and lightning, not even letting in periods of sunshine. The open drainage gutter begins to swell, so my chickens are getting soaked, nowhere to keep dry. Mama puts more layers of metal sheeting on the roof of the coop to keep the rain out and also covers the wire mesh with plastic. I do not like to see my chickens like this…. They are dying, swept away by the swollen gutter. I rescue as many as I can, but my chicken population is slowly depleting. But from what is to follow, my chicken population does not matter.

⇒⇐

The eight-week holiday is drawing to a close, and I begin to fret about Ngozi. I do not look forward to going back to school. A week before the new term, I am turning the handle of the Singer sewing machine and Mama says, 'Tolani'.

'Yes, Mama?' I reply without stopping to fix the snagged stitching.

'You will be going to live with Mummy in Ikoyi and will be starting a new school', Mama says.

I stop in the middle of completing a full turn of the handle, taking this great news with mixed feelings. I am happy that I will not be seeing Ngozi again but sad that I will be leaving Mama. 'But Mama, I don't want to go and live with Mummy, I want to stay here with you, and who will look after my chickens, Mama?'

Mama stops, sensing the sadness in my voice. 'Tolani, my child, it is only for a short while'.

I feel the sadness in Mama's voice, which does not reassure me that all is well.

'And…' she continues, 'your school is too far. It is in Victoria Island, and I will not be able to take you there'.

Actually, the news does not seem bad, I think in my head. *A new school, living with Mummy.* Actually, going back to live with my mother and father, perhaps I am not a 'bastard child' after all. I have seen Mummy visit Mama several times, and on such occasions I am asked to leave the parlour while she and Mama talk. Mummy is Mama's daughter and walks with such graceful-ness, well dressed and heeled. But Mummy never pays any attention to me and says nothing to me except to acknowledge my greeting. So I wonder why I am going to live with her, but anyway, that is a thought for another day.

The day to leave the bungalow of Obalende arrives. 'Don't pack too many clothes', Mama says to me, but I pack my favourites—the blue dress Mama and I made, and my red and black patent Dolly shoes— in a well-used, vintage brown suitcase that fits only a few clothes. I make my way to the backyard, hoping to catch a glimpse of Tunde or Ade and tell of my departure, but no one is there. I scoop a handful of grain and scatter it around me so that I am surrounded by my chickens. I hold back tears. I will miss watching all of this. They are oblivious about my departure. I take one last look at the backyard, run my hand over the pitanga tree and the bitter leaf plant, and shut the backyard gate behind me with a big sigh.

I stand holding the suitcase, waiting for Mama to give me a hug, but she averts her eyes from mine. 'Bye-bye, Tolani. Be a good girl'.

I do not reply. I know something is wrong, but I do not have the time to cry, and I dare not throw a tantrum. I follow Mummy and get into the big brown car, taking in one last look at the street lined with bungalows, watching my friends playing and waving at me. But I do not return the wave as I stifle my tears. And slowly, the big brown car leaves the streets of Obalende, past the bustling noise of the bus depot where Mama and I boarded the different routes on shared journeys, shared moments. Still I refuse to let the tears fall. I am on a journey to discover what lies at the end of my rainbow.

CHAPTER THREE

We leave the hustle and the rather noisy Obalende streets behind and slowly pull into a much quieter area of Ikoyi. There is a significant difference. The streets are wider, and not many people are around, even for a Saturday afternoon—just an occasional person on a bicycle. The streets are lined with lots of trees. Some are huge trees with wide trunks, while some have thin trunks, and there are lots of palm trees. I catch a glimpse of a big house tucked far back, hidden by the thick foliage of the huge trees, as if they are shielding the inhabitants from the outside.

Tick, tick, tick, Mummy slows down, indicating left into a front gate and driving slowly on the gravel driveway. The journey has been very quiet Mummy has not said a word to me she appears much focused and I sense a feeling of apprehension in her mannerisms with her long drawn sighs. Revealing before me a huge white building, just one of the many Colonial buildings that now serves as official accommodation for the most senior civil servants surrounded by palm trees, neatly cut grass, and a gravel driveway. She pulls to a stop in a garage. She motions to me to get down and follow her. I look around, trying to take in the size of the building and my new environment. I can actually experience what Bintu Mama's house help must have felt like coming to live with Mama in Obalende from her village, with her whole life's belongings in her hands.

Mummy motions, but I stay just outside a door that is soon to yield its secrets. After a brief moment, a girl comes and asks that I follow her. 'Put your case there. Come with me'. She leads the way to the outbuilding, boys' quarters, where she shows me the shower room with a bucket full of some solution that smells vile. Mummy says I have to bathe with that Pointing at the bucket, Mummy says, 'It will get rid of any craw-craw or any hidden diseases you are carrying with you'.

I do as I am told. I undress to bathe with the vile-smelling solution of 'Izal'—yes, that's what it's called. Mama often asked Bintu to use it to disinfect the bathroom and toilet. I take a look at my brown skin from the only glint of light coming through the crack in the washroom window. Examining myself closely, I do not have any craw-craw; Mama makes sure of that and moisturises my body with lashings and lashings of shea butter. From what I was taught at school, craw-craw is some skin disease, but I do not carry craw-craw—or any skin disease, for that matter. Hesitantly, I pour the Izal over my body, still welcoming the cold afternoon shower after sitting in the hot car for the journey. 'Take this. Put it on', the girl says, handing me an oversized blue dress, so long it covers up my ankles. We both make our way to the big house.

'Take off your slippers', she says. 'You are not allowed slippers in the house'. I follow her through a large carpeted hallway. The carpet seems to cushion my feet; it feels soft and gives way as we make our way along. Up the stairs I go with my suitcase, through a set of double doors opening up to a landing, and then a sharp left through another set of doors. In there is a mighty bedroom with wooden floors. Pieces of cut-out boards are intricately arranged to form a pattern. The huge windows have heavy curtains draping from the top right to the floor. In the middle of this huge room sits a huge bed on the soft, luxurious carpet. The bed is bigger than the one I shared with Mama. It could accommodate all the friends I played with on the street. The bed has crisp white bed sheets and does not look like it has been slept in today. Adjoining this room are two smaller rooms, and the girl leads me to one of them. 'Put your things down and sit', she says, showing me a woven cane chair propped up beside the oak dressing table. I do as I am told, and she leaves, closing the door behind her.

I look round the room. It's bigger than the one I shared with Mama. It has the same huge windows as the bigger room, but with a different colour of curtains. They drape from the very top of the ceiling to the floor. The room has French double doors. In the far corner of the room is a small bed, looking very lonely. It is made up, but not in white sheets. I become a bit unsettled, not sure what to make of my new surroundings. Perhaps I should have protested loudly to Mama, and maybe she would not have made me come.

The door opens, and the girl says Mummy is calling me. On the way down the stairs, I ask her name. 'Pe-ne-lo-pe'. She speaks each syllable of her name slowly. 'My name is Tolani', I say.

Penelope has a big build, a bit like Ngozi, but she looks a year younger than me. Looking at her, I do not think we are related. I do not think she is my sister; in fact, I do not think Mummy is my real mother.

That weekend gives me an opportunity to fully take in the grandness of the house, painted white inside and outside with red patio cement floors on every side that shine in the afternoon sun. It looks exactly like I have seen in pictures of some of the grand parties

Mama attended with the wives of the Colonial masters. That weekend, I am introduced to 'rules': no shouting, no talking loudly, no running, and…wait for it… bells. Yes, bells. Each one of us has bell rings assigned to us, in order of seniority. One ring of the bell is for Monsieur Garcon, the cook; two are for his deputy; three are for me; and four are for Penelope. There are no other children, no sleeping babies—just me and… no, wait—there is also Chief, Mummy's Husband.

Both Penelope and I greet Chief, kneeling down to the figure that is looking out of the dining room window with his back turned to us. From what I can make out from the standing figure, Chief is a big man with a bulging belly. With a wave of her hand, Mummy dismisses us from the kneeling position, and we make our way to sit outside the kitchen and watch Monsieur Garcon prepare the evening meal. That space outside of the kitchen becomes base for Penelope and me. And true to the rules of the house, one bell ring signals supper. Monsieur Garcon wheels in the trolley laden with a variety of courses, very different from the bitter leaf and egusi soup or okra soup Mama and I shared together. I try not to look too hard, but it looks quite mouth-watering.

'Vien ici, asseyez vous', Monsieur Garcon calls in French to serve us supper. I look at Penelope, confused.

'Come, it's time for us to eat', she says.

Supper is a bowl of Agidi, with spinach. Yuk! Agidi is a popular Nigerian dish made with corn flour. I hate Agidi, and Mama never gave it to me. I close my eyes and say grace. 'God bless this food, bless the hands that cooked this food, bless the hands that provided the food, and God bless Mummy and Chief'. With that, I slowly eat what is before me, trying to hold back the tears. Mama taught me to be always grateful for whatever I am given to eat and not waste food.

Sunday is no different from the day before. I am expecting to go to church, but that does not happen. I use this opportunity to get to know more about Penelope and her relevance to Mummy and the white house. Penelope stays silent on all the questions I am asking and cleverly changes the subject, instead asking about me. But I do not trust her, either, and keep my not-long-ago past to myself. I am thinking, *How can I coexist with Penelope when we don't trust each other and know nothing about each other?* But I am able to establish the relationships among everyone in the white house, and the future will have to prove me right or wrong.

CHAPTER FOUR

'Tolani, you'd better hurry up and take your bath before Mummy comes up and whips you with the koboko if you're not in bed', Penelope says.

'What?' I look at her with disbelief. 'Koboko', I repeat, picturing a long whip made of animal skin.

'Yes, and you will get the whipping tonight if you keep standing there', she adds.

I hurriedly take my shower in the en suite bathroom adjoining Penelope's bedroom, then rush to the safety of my bedroom—no more conversation. I say my prayers as I have been taught in Sunday School. 'Dear God, bless Mama, Mummy, and Chief. God, keep Penelope and me, and prepare me for my day at my new school tomorrow'. My prayer is interrupted by Mummy's soft, padding footsteps. I quickly jump up and tuck myself in bed, in fear of the koboko.

'You'. I am awoken by Mummy's voice in the room that I am still getting accustomed to.

'Good morning, Ma'.

'This is your school uniform and bag', she says.

'Thank you, Ma'.

She closes the door behind her. The crisp, new school uniform is white with a short-sleeved blouse, grey pinafore, and panama hat. This is totally different from my previous local school. Going by the uniform, I already feel different. I steal a look at myself in the standing mirror in Mummy's dressing room, which now doubles as my bedroom.

The door opens again, and Penelope beckons. I follow her, tiptoeing out through Mummy's bedroom because Chief is still asleep—well, I actually think he is pretending to be asleep.

Breakfast is a piping-hot bowl of pap; corn flour porridge I say my grace. The food is too hot, and it does not help that Monsieur Garcon is hurrying us up because Baba Kareem is waiting to take us to school. He hands us both a sandwich, and Penelope and I hurriedly put on school shoes, grab identical school bags, and make a dash for the car park, not wanting to incur the wrath of Mummy for keeping Baba Kareem waiting. Baba Kareem walks with a slight limp as he lets us in the Clubman.

Over time, the journeys in the Clubman come to be where Penelope and I get to know and trust each other, and I get to find out more about her. The journeys in the Clubman give both Penelope and me the freedom to be children with a sense of escape. They also are when Baba Kareem tells us distressing but very interesting stories about the civil war, how he came face-to-face with enemies, and tactics he employed to defeat the enemy. 'You see, I have three bullets in my leg', he says.

'But Baba Kareem', I ask, 'how can someone still be alive with three bullets in his leg?'

'I have a very powerful charm Juju; it's called that even no bullet can harm me; and that's a fact'

I am full of admiration for Baba Kareem's bravery and just can't imagine what dreadful things he must have had to do and watch, all in the name of war. Sometimes we find his stories entertaining on the journeys; they make us forget the overcast shadows of the mood at the white house.

My school, as Mama had said, is one of the best international schools in the leafy suburbs of Victoria Island.

'This is Tolani'. I am introduced to the class of boys and girls.

'Hello, Tolani', the class choruses.

Not knowing how to reply, I say nothing.

'Uchenna, Tolani will be your partner. She will sit next to you', the teacher, Mrs Grillo, says, and she shows me to my desk beside Uchenna. Uchenna has a fat, round face and looks friendly. Mrs Grillo speaks with crisp English, totally different from the pidgin English in my former local school. I feel nervous about how I will fit in and be able to speak like the other children. I wish Mama were here to reassure me. My thoughts are broken by the voice of Mrs Grillo announcing that we are having a math test. Oh, no! Math is not one of my favourite subjects, and here I am on my first day in a new school facing a test. All the other children seem to know the workings as all heads are down, working away at the sums on the board. I try to see what Uchenna is writing, but she cleverly shields her work. God, I am stuck, but I pretend to work away, not wanting to be left out.

At playtime, Uchenna is quite friendly and walks me around the school grounds, white sand that gives way under our sandals. She shows me the swimming pool, the swings, and all sorts of playground equipment. Wow! My lunch is a bread and butter sandwich. I look at Uchenna's lunch bag; she has a lunch meal in her bag that is enough for two people. No wonder she has fat cheeks, with all that food! She offers me a bit of cake, which I gladly accept, as I am still a bit hungry after devouring my sandwich.

Afternoon lessons come with new things to learn and more tests. I do my best, but being new to these topics, I know my performance is one of the poorest in the class. When school ends, Penelope comes looking for me, and we both wait with the other children at the gate for Baba Kareem.

'Good afternoon, Ma'. Both Penelope and I greet Mummy, who is standing by the kitchen-door entrance. We receive no acknowledgment. Twak, twak, twak! The Koboko whip unleashes on me. 'You Olodo girl. You're so stupid!' Mummy says. 'Simple math you can't even do'. The lashings continue. 'You can't amount to anything. C'mon, get out of my sight'. I scramble to gather my books and bag that had gotten flung in different directions on the sand.

In the safety of the bedroom, I examine the welts on my arm, where the whip caught my left cheek, my legs. I keep myself from crying from the stings and try to figure out how Mummy found out about how badly I performed on the test. I pass on dinner that evening and empty my bowl into Penelope's. She wolfs it down without having any sympathy for what has befallen me. The cold shower provides some comfort on the welts, as it soothes them and calms the stinging for a bit. And as I kneel down to say the Lord's Prayer, I can no longer hold in the tears. They overwhelm me. I sob on my knees and cry myself to sleep. I want to go back to Mama!

The next few weeks at school, I spend lunchtime with Mrs Grillo, who is giving me extra lessons in math and diction. 'Teacher, not tesha. Kitchen, not kishen. Chair, not shia. Chicken, not shiken', she instructs. I must have really done badly on the test for Mrs Grillo to be giving up her lunchtime to make sure I am at the same level as the other children. The day of my encounter with the whip, I promised myself that it would be the last. I make more effort in class to learn. I even surprise my French teacher with how quickly I have progressed. Well, I must give the thanks to Monsieur Garcon, who speaks to Penelope and me in French while waiting for dinner in the kitchen. I mimic Mrs Grillo's pronunciations, her 'Queen's English', and gain more confidence in my new school. I am beginning to like Mrs Grillo!

'Au revoir, Monsieur Garcon!' I say one day.

'Au revoir, Tolani et Penelope. Ont une bonne journee!'

We head down the gravel drive to meet Baba Kareem for another interesting journey to school.

'Why don't you like playing with the other children?' I ask Uchenna as we sit to eat lunch.

'They are not kind to me', she replies. 'They call me "fatty bom bom"!' Looking at her lunch box filled with a meat pie, cake, a doughnut, and a Samco chocolate drink, I hold myself back from laughing and think, *Uchenna does have a pudgy face and fat cheeks. With all the food she eats, enough for two people, it is not surprising*. But she is lovely and friendly. Uchenna tells me about her family. Her father is a businessman who travels abroad a lot for business deals in the export of oil. She has six siblings.

'What? There are seven children in the house?' I ask.

'Yes, seven of us'.

'Wow, I wish I had brothers and sisters, too', I say. 'And I wish I lived with my mum and dad'. I feel a lump well in my throat, so I quickly change the subject.

But Uchenna continues, 'And we go to the club on Saturdays to watch films. Have you been to the club?'

'No', I say. *And I don't think I will be going anytime soon*, I think.

CHAPTER FIVE

During the half-term holiday, we have nothing to do. We spend the afternoons sitting idle in the shade of the porch, away from the heat of the day, or stealing conversations with Monsieur Garcon's wife, Genevieve, at the boys quarters stewards sleeping accommodation.

'You both', Mummy summons. 'Take those baskets and wash all the plates and cutlery. Make sure you don't break any of the glasses'.

The chore is welcome, as it occupies us for the rest of the day. Mummy is preparing for Chief's fiftieth birthday party celebration. Of course, we can't help being caught up in the sudden excitement and urgency of what needs to be done before the big day.

'Penelope, do you think we are going to get the new aso Ebi attire, made from the same identical fabric for us?'

'I don't know', I say. I go on to describe the style I want mine made into. Because I am distracted, I carelessly drop a plate, and it comes crashing into smithereens. Before I can even gather myself, Mummy appears with the Koboko. Penelope is caught in the frenzy as it lands. When it is over, we both burst out laughing—at what, I don't know, but it makes it less painful if I laugh. But my...was it painful!

On party day, Penelope and I are given firm instructions to stay on the porch and keep watch over the caterers so that they don't siphon food away. We are not to go anywhere near the party. Monsieur Garcon will see to all our needs for the day. I creep to the front of the house on hearing the arrival of the guests. I am waiting and watching and hoping that Mama will come. But Mama is not coming, I realise, and I tire of watching. I return to the porch to see Penelope at the wire fence by the stewards sleeping accommodation. On the other side of the fence is a white girl not much older than both of us, and I make my approach.

'Hello', I say, and I join in the conversation. Before we know what is happening, White Girl squeezes herself through an opening in the wire fence and comes over.

'Is there a party going on?' she asks. 'Can I come and have a look?'

'No! No!' we shout in horror, trying to keep her from venturing farther into the compound, fearful of what will happen.

'Let's just stay here and talk'.

Between sips of Fanta and plates of assorted meat that Monsieur Garcon makes sure we are in good supply of, and him, too, we make a new friendship with White Girl until her nanny comes calling for her, and we bid our good-byes.

'See you again'.

The parties held at the white house are lavish—cocktail parties, dinner parties, and parties 'just because we can afford it'. Each has pretty much the same routine of preparation, and we are banished to the boys' quarter porch. The parties actually are a blessing in disguise because we forge a relationship with White Girl. During such parties, we venture into her home through the gap in the fence, into a well-manicured garden. Adorning the centre is a wide swimming pool that seems to beckon us in the afternoon heat. She takes us to her playroom, her nanny in tow. She asks the nanny, 'Angela, please, can we watch *Chitty Chitty Bang Bang*?'

To me, she says, 'You will enjoy this movie'.

'Do cars really fly in London?' I ask.

'Sshhh', White Girl says to quiet me. 'It's only make-believe. There are no such things as flying cars'.

The film takes us into a world of happy adventure and leaves me wishing I were Jemima Potts.

In the stolen moments at White Girl's house, I am introduced to comic-book characters like Asterix, Tin Tin, and Snowy and the Adventure and Beano comics, which seem to shut out the sadness of the white house, though briefly.

The Common Entrance Selection exams are approaching, and with the progress I have made, I am sure I will gain admission into one of the selective secondary schools on the island. If I don't, I guess I will have another unpleasant meeting with the leather whip.

'Tolani, I am going to a boarding school', Uchenna tells me one day. It's a boarding school in Enugu.

'Won't you miss your brothers and sisters?' I ask.

'Not really, because we have a house in Enugu, and they will be visiting. I, too, will be allowed to go home'.

I toy with the Idea of going to a boarding school away from the white house, but Mummy has chosen my school.

'Coup! Coup! Coup!' Our afternoon preparation for the exams is shattered by the panicked voices of parents at the school gates. The head of state has been assassinated, this is a bloody coup, people are being killed, and panic-stricken parents are rushing through the gates to fetch their children. When the rebels take over the TV station, even more panic sets in, and I can see the helplessness of the teachers. Panic overtakes the whole school, which is right next to the broadcasting house. In the melee of the panic, Penelope sees me at the gate waiting for Baba Kareem. Baba Kareem tries to make us calm, seeing the panic in our eyes, but his words and his voice do not sound reassuring. He is probably fearing the worst, having been out of the Nigerian Civil War not long himself. But he drives on, weaving in and out of traffic, speeding at breakneck speed past army cars blaring their sirens on the streets of Ikoyi. Finally we reach the safety of the white house.

Chief does not return that night, and I can hear Mummy on the telephone, panic in her voice, as she rings 'round, trying to find the whereabouts of Chief. She is able to establish that he and some other senior civil servants have been arrested for fraudulent activities while in office and incarcerated in Alagbon Prisons. Mummy becomes more irritable over the next few days, and we make sure to be well out of her way— not that we see much of her; she is out early in the morning 'til curfew time trying to gain Chief's release. So we are left in the care of Monsieur Garcon. Well, I will say it's a blessing in disguise because we are left to idle even more, and we gain more confidence through more rendezvous with our new friend, White Girl.

During Mummy's absences from the house to see to Chief's release and take him food, Baba Kareem tells me about Alagbon Prisons—appallingly unsanitary conditions and inhumane treatment, and food is even a luxury. I wonder how Chief will survive under those conditions.

Whenever Mummy leaves in the morning, in comes Mr Palmi, an old, fragile-looking man but with the energy of a young man. I come to understand that Mr Palmi has a deal with Monsieur Garcon, allowing him to come and tap the palm trees. In exchange, he gives Monsieur Garcon some Naira notes. I can't stop watching in amazement at the skill and dexterity with which he ascends each tree. He seems to know what each individual tree will yield. He comes back down with the gourd full, firmly strapped to his waistband. Penelope and I have our first taste of fermented palm wine. We experience the feeling of drunkenness, and in a strange way. We look forward to Mr Palmi's visits. Bad…very bad, but who's watching? Not even Monsieur Garcon seems to care. Penelope's drunkenness unleashes silliness; she runs in circles around the rubber tree and in and out of the pineapple grove until she tires herself out. Mine is a bit more melancholy. When I am drunk, I recall tales of living with Mama, think about how I miss my chickens, and wonder if there are any left. I even show some James Brown moves to Genevieve, Monsieur Garcon's wife. I fill up with giggles, then descend into little sobs 'til I have no more tears to shed—in between, still sipping the palm wine.

When not drunk with Palmi, I learn some more French from Genevieve, and by now I am able to hold simple conversations with her.

'Genevieve, se il vous plait, me montre comment tresser cornrow'. ' Genevieve, please show me how to braid cornrow,

'Oui, bien sur, Penelope.; " O Yes, of course, Tolani'

'venez regarder comme je Penelope natt de Cheveuse'. Genevieve tells me to come watch her plait Penelope's hair.

And with several practice sessions with Penelope's hair, I graduate from fat doo-doo plats to perfecting tidy cornrows on my own hair.

The weeks go by, and Chief is still not released. I sometimes hear Mummy crying at night, and I just want to reach out to her and tell her everything will be fine and that Chief will be home safely. But I dare not. My heart wants to reach out, but my head tells me, *Remember the leather whip.* I pray for Chief to be home safely and soon.

Several weeks later, one early morning, while waiting for Baba Kareem at the gravel drive, an army van drives in, no sirens blaring, It parks by the main door, and the occupant steps out. I take a second look. It is Chief—not in buba and sokoto, a traditional apparel worn by men, but in some simple trousers and a shirt. Chief is looking frail and certainly appears to have shrunk; the protruding belly has disappeared. Mama comes rushing out of the door, overjoyed at his release, and we go to school. Unsurprisingly, there is another preparation for another lavish party, celebrating Chief's release.

After this last party, things are about to change in the white house. Monsieur Garcon is sacked; he has been caught pilfering foodstuff from Mummy's pantry. It is a sad moment for me in particular, as I have quite taken to Monsieur Garcon and his wife, who taught me how to put my Afro in plats, which I perfected, ensuring that my hair was always in neat plats for school. I have come to like Monsieur Garcon like family and will surely miss him and his wife.

The results of the Common Entrance Exam are published, and I have gained admission to one of the best Catholic secondary schools on the island. I feel proud of myself that I will not have to face the wrath of Mummy with the leather whip. Uchenna is even more elated, as she is going to her selected boarding school in Enugu, where she will be joining her cousins.

So we part ways...with no exchange of telephone numbers or addresses. I do not write hers down because I know I have no use for the information. I do not provide information to her, either—not that I have it anyway. The last thing Mrs Grillo tells me is, 'Go find what's at the end of your rainbow'.

CHAPTER SIX

Monsieur Garcon is not replaced, but Mummy takes over the cooking, and Penelope and I are given the responsibilities of looking after this big house and doing chores that need carrying out, both before and after school. The only saving grace is we do not have to do the heavy washing; a washerman is employed to wash Chief's now oversized Agbadas, a long, flowing robe with wide sleeves.

We are locked indoors for most of the day, from when Mummy goes to work until she gets back to prepare the evening meal. Then we stand in the kitchen to wash up and have dinner. We no longer see White

Girl because we have not been able to go to the back fence since Monsieur Garcon left.

Penelope and I quickly get used to the routines. We lose our personalities and have no names; we are summoned by the three or four rings of the bell or 'you two'. 'You two', Mummy summons, and she hands me some money and gives us directions to my secondary school tailor. I need to get fitted for my new school uniform. Inside, I am excited because for the first time in weeks, we are going out and on our own. This is fantastic, going out on our own and taking the bus to town. I feel like Chief must have felt on his release from Alagbon, but I feel even more excitement, which I hide while listening to instructions from Mummy. 'Yes, Ma', I say, and we depart promptly before she changes her mind. On the bus journey, a bad thought fills my head: *Maybe I should just run away and never return*. But where to? And with Penelope in tow, no; we may both end up in the hands of kidnappers. Mama told me about kidnappers, how children are never seen again, and no one knows what tragedy has befallen them.

Secondary school creates new trepidations and anxieties. Will I fit in? How will I cope with making new friends? I guess I have to find out when I get there. I wait at the bus stop in my new, crisp uniform for the right bus to come along.

The girls are mostly from army parentage and are transported to school accompanied by a soldier or some sort of security. The first day is not a good start. The class manages to get a whole-class punishment for giggling when a teacher is speaking. We are all made to kneel on the gravel drive in the hot sun, sweating. I hate it. Some of the girls who know each other are talking of making a report to their parents and saying how the teacher will be given a telling off. I just want to be out of the sun so I don't sweat so much in my new uniform! Mummy does not like sweaty people; she says they stink like rotten meat. Now, thanks to these immature, over-pampered girls, I have her wrath to look forward to.

Cliques are quickly formed in the first few weeks— girls who go to the club Uchenna told me about, girls who went to the same primary school, girls whose parents are friends, or just girls who are from the same over-pampered background. What I find most amusing is the idea that one needs to be looked after by a senior student, the school daughter/school mother. Well, of course no one approaches me to be their school daughter—not that I am disappointed. I just wonder what the whole idea is about. But I find a friend in Honey.

Not that I have much in common in Honey, either, but we are not cool enough to belong to any of the cliques. Honey tells me she is newly arrived from London and how her parents came back to live in Nigeria with her siblings. They live in Ajegunle.

'So why did your parents bring you back to Nigeria?' I ask, not that it makes any difference to me. I just want to know more about her life in London.

'You see, we lived in a Council Housing Estate in Dalston', she explains. 'My dad is an engineer and could not find a good job. Mum works as a cleaner, but I think it's got something to do with "papers", and my dad decides he's had enough. So here we are'.

'Are you going back sometime soon?' I ask, thinking quietly for my own selfish reasons.

'No, my dad has gotten a job working with Shell, and my Mom is a teacher'.

'Do you like it here in Nigeria?' I ask.

'Sometimes, but I miss my friends on the estate. We are never going back, as I have heard my dad say to my mum. It's very noisy in Ajegunle, but I am getting used to the noise and hustle and bustle'.

⚊⊹ ⊹⚊

Festac 77 is here. The nation is excited about the Festival of Arts and Culture. Nigeria is hosting several performing artist from other African nations. Several shows and performances are held at the newly built arts theatre.

'Did you see Ipi-Tombi last night on TV?' Wuraola, another classmate asks Honey and me. She proceeds to demonstrate a rather complex dance routine, almost keeling over.

'No, and who are they?' I answer.

'Ah! You mean you haven't seen Ipi-Tombi? Don't you watch telly?'

I brace myself from the tirade of words lurking at the tip of my tongue; I feel irritated by the question for some reason.

She continues, 'OK, did you watch Kinta Kunte?'

Really, now I am very irritated. 'Shut up!' I snap. 'Who cares about any Ipi-Tombi or Kinta-Kunte, and who called you over here with your stupidity?'

I am stopped from further unleashing my tirade of anger on her because the bell rings to indicate that the lunch period is over. I don't know what came over me. The girls just assume that everyone is privileged to watch TV. There is a TV in the white house, but Penelope and I are forbidden to sit and watch. We only catch a glimpse of what's on during our chores in and out of Mummy's room. Festac is now over, Kinta-Kunte is over, but somehow I become fascinated by snippets of what's happening to Kinta-Kunte when Honey gives an update at lunchtime. She never asks why I don't watch TV, and as long as she respects that, our friendship will survive.

Since the release of Chief from Alagbon Prisons, we seem to hear more of him in the evenings. He seems to be on the phone all evening until dinner is served. We do the same after-school routine chores: set the table for Chief, serve dinner to Chief, clear the plates for Chief, prepare a hand-washing basin for Chief.

'Good evening, sir'. 'Good night, sir'. We receive no acknowledgment but still do the same daily routine. I don't even know if Chief knows our names, but I suppose there is no reason for him to.

While waiting for Mummy to come downstairs to prepare the evening meal, we see White Girl by the wire fence, our rendezvous point. She knows not to venture into the compound since the departure of Monsieur Garcon; in fact, we have not been to her house since Monsieur Garcon's departure. It was too risky. Penelope and I steal this opportunity to have a chat through the fence, and White Girl announces, 'We are going to live in Hong Kong. My dad has gotten a job at the embassy in Hong Kong, and we leave tomorrow night. I have not been able to tell you because I have not seen you'.

My heart becomes weakened, and I immediately want to cry. She pushes comic books through the fence and says, 'Take these'.

'No, sorry, I can't take them', I reply. 'Please, you must go now. Good-bye'.

I turn away quickly, holding back tears. I will miss White Girl. I have lost a friend.

The chores do not get any easier; carrying water up the stairs really tires my arms. Yes! Fetching pails and pails of water to supply the three bathrooms in the house, though I wonder who uses the third one. It still remains a mystery to me. It is necessary to fetch the pails of water because Nigeria, post-oil boom, 'post-Udoji'. Ahh...yes. Chief Udoji awards salary increases for all civil servants. During the 'dollar booming oil' economy, infrastructure and basic amenities have been neglected in the squander of wealth by the privileged—Chief included—so the nation suffers from power cuts and water shortages.

As I make my way up the stairs trying not to spill water on the wooden floor, I wonder if Mama knows and what will she say. Knowing how she imbibed a hard-work value in me, she will probably say, 'My child, it is for your own good', but the handles of the heavy metal pail hurt my arms really badly.

CHAPTER SEVEN

An argument erupts at break time between Onyekachi and Jane. This is quite unusual, as Onyekachi is very quiet, so the reason for this argument is baffling. The girls mill around to listen to the gist of the argument. Apparently, Onyekachi was seen speaking to Kofo at the 'club', and Jane likes Kofo. The argument goes on and on. I try so hard not to laugh, but it is very funny how two girls can be having an argument over this boy. For what reason? What a waste of time. I grab Honey and walk to the library to poke more fun about Kofo, Jane, and Onyekachi.

'Tolani, Tolani! Wait, wait!' Jane comes running to catch up with Honey and me as we make our way to Friday-morning mass. She hands me a card; it's an invitation to her twelfth birthday party, which will be at the club. Yes, the same exclusive club where children of the rich and affluent meet over the weekends, the same club Uchenna told me about. Now Jane is inviting me to her party there. I become quite excited about being invited, but I take a closer look at the neat handwriting on the card and can't help but notice that my name has been etched over some scratched-out name—Onyekachi's. So I have been invited on second thoughts, which dampens my excitement. Not that I will be going, but all the same, it hurts me to have been considered on second thoughts. 'Thank you, Jane'.

'Will you come? Please say you will come, Tolani'.

'Yes, Jane. I will come', I say, just to make her go away. My sadness is divided in two—first I am sad for Honey that she has not been invited, and second I am sad for me that even though I was invited, it was as a 'replacement'. The chance of me attending is nil. And with that, I throw the card in the nearest bin and forget all about it.

Not surprisingly, on Monday morning, the girls are all talking about how fantastic Jane's party was, how much fun was had, and about the gifts they had in their goody bags. Funny how Jane does not ask why I did not go. Well, I am not surprised; we are not really friends after all. Jane's party invitation is the first and last I ever get, as it becomes clear to the girls whose parents threw parties for them, 'Why waste an "after-thought"' party invitation on Tolani?'

My twelfth birthday comes up, and I will now officially be an adult. But what comes with adulthood, and what really changes? No birthday present, no birthday party, not even an acknowledgment of the special day from Mummy. I find myself saying to Penelope on the way to school, 'It's my birthday today, you know?'

'Happy birthday, Tolani'.

'Thank you', I reply, which prompts me to mention the subject I have been wondering about: 'Penelope, you have not told me how you came to live in the white house'.

'Well…after I arrived from London with my parents and older brother, my mother decided that I would come and live with Mummy and Chief, as she says it's much better for me. My mother has not visited since she brought me to the white house, and I really do miss my family'.

For the first time, I see Penelope break down and cry, and I feel sorry for her. 'Don't worry, Penelope. I am sure your mother has not forgotten you. She will come someday. Maybe she's just trying to sort some things out and then will come and take you back to live with her'. The words are not very comforting, but that's all I can offer. I needed comforting that morning myself but settle for speaking comforting words to Penelope.

I think I am starting to reach puberty, according to the biology lesson in class today. For most of the girls, this is not new to them, as they have already hit puberty—you know, the works: bra wearing, periods, sanitary towels, and all that. I am also beginning to notice some changes to my body shape. My breasts are growing bigger, and I am growing hair in places that had no hair before. I feel scared about these changes, unsure of what to do. I need to see Mama; she will know. She will tell me what to do. Puberty did arrive faster than I thought, and my periods frighten me the most. I rely on Honey for supplies; she is experiencing the same changes. I can't tell Mummy; I am too scared. If I can just stop the hands of puberty from happening, I will gladly do so.

As I clear remnants of food from Chief's plate, suddenly he lunges forward and grabs at my breast. Startled, I jump back, dropping the dish with its half-eaten contents on the floor. The clamour of the smashed dish brings Mummy from the kitchen, and lo! That koboko seems to know just when to appear. 'You foolish, good-for-nothing girl!' Mummy screams, the leather whip landing and tearing away at the flesh on my face, arms, all over my body. I abandon trying to clear up the broken dishes and am banished to stand outside, far from the sight of Mummy. As I sit by the garage, I put my head between my knees, sobbing quietly and praying that it will not rain so hard....

Mummy starts attending Holy Charismatic prayers at the local Catholic church in the evenings after dinner is served and leaves Penelope and me at home in separate rooms. We dare venture out and are bold enough to turn the TV on and catch a glimpse of the evening news. It's easy to know when Mummy arrive, as we hear the approach of tyre on the gravel drive. Or sometimes Penelope will come to my room, and we chat about nothing of any importance. Just being able to have a chat before Mummy comes back is nice.

One evening, after Mummy goes to church, tired and slumped over my textbook, dozing in and out of sleep, I hear creeping footsteps on the floorboards. They are not the hurried footsteps of Penelope, and I wonder who it is, as Mummy is out. The door opens, and I look up. There is Chief, standing: 'a gentleman in the proper'. I quickly avert my eyes and stammer, 'Good evening, sir'.

'Come', he says, and I follow, not having time to wonder what for. Since I have been in the house, this is the first word Chief has spoken to me. I follow him to his wing of the bedroom and hesitate outside of the room, as we are never allowed in Chief's room—only under the watchful eyes of Mummy to sweep, dust, and polish the wooden floors. Chief, seeing my hesitation, pulls me inside, kicks the door shut, drags me to the bed, and slams me onto the bed, onto the white crisp linen bed sheet we are forbidden to even touch. His heaving body on top of me, I feel his hardness against me. I feel his hardness inside of me, tearing through my body, and he is grunting harder, harder, faster, faster. I close my eyes, clench my teeth against the pain. I cannot scream. Harder and harder he grunts, and 'Ooooh!' He lets out a soft moan, rolls off of me, and pushes me onto the floor. Blinded by the pain, I search for my pants and try to run. My feet keel under me from the crippling pain, almost making me buckle over. I feel stickiness between my thighs.

In the relative safety of my bedroom, I examine my body—blood! This means injury; I have been injured. Panic takes over the pain. Chief has injured me, and if this bleeding is not treated, I will probably bleed to death slowly in this room and die before the morning. I grab my towel to wipe off the blood. I wipe so hard that my inner thighs begin to sting. I need to take a shower, but how can I explain an afternoon shower to Penelope, and more so, if caught while in the shower by Mummy, how can I explain that? I try to sit on the cane chair. The pain shoots through my body. I think of sitting on the bed, but I will bleed all over the bed, and I can't explain it to Mummy—that is, if I don't die before then. I roll up my towel to form a cushion and sit on it gently to ease the pain. I sit quietly trying to fathom what just happened and wondering how I can tell anyone what just happened.

I hear footsteps again, the same slow, calculated footsteps approaching the room. Chief enters. I do not move from my sitting position. He approaches slowly. He pulls me up from the chair with both hands and holds me close to his chest, now clothed in a crisp white, flowing agbada. I hear his slow heartbeat, as if calming and assuring me that everything will be fine. I stand frozen, trying not to be overtaken by his cologne, 'Brut for Men'. Yes, that's his cologne, as I have seen on his dressing table while tidying up his room. Slowly he lifts my hand and gently places in it a crisp note, then lets me go and shuts the door behind him. Still standing, I take a look at the note: 50 Naira! A 50-Naira note! I have never seen, much less been given that much money, ever, even when I was living with Mama. I become excited and begin to calculate how to spend the money. The pain shoots right through my body, reminding me of my injury. Will Penelope believe me if I tell her?

That night, as I kneel down to pray, I asked God for Chief not to injure me anymore, for Mummy to stop using the koboko, and for me to pass my exams…lights out.

Over the next couple of days, I become very popular. I can afford to buy food for both myself and Penelope, and I treat Honey and other 'friends' to food—'Mama Put' a breakfast of rice and assorted meat. I place orders of breakfast for my friends, oya! 'Mama Put'

I tell the rice vendor, Serve us rice and meat and soft drinks. I make my orders on the queue, holding out the tin plates. Lessons also seem more interesting, and my friends look forward to lunch time, when I buy a gala meat pie, which we down with mineral water. Neither Penelope nor Honey ask how I suddenly came into money, but I am bent to enjoy it while it lasts.

I can also afford to buy my own sanitary supplies and do not have to depend on the kind generosity of Honey. So while Mummy attends her Holy Charismatic session, Chief engages me in his 'unholy charismatic sessions', but in each session, he chats to me about issues that are of no relevance to me. I lie there on the crisp white linen sheets with my eyes closed, just listening. 'Brown-skinned girl' is what he calls me, though I am not surprised, as he never speaks to Penelope and me, so he probably does not know what my name is. 'Brown-skinned girl', he says, 'the contractor on site is cheating me out of cement and blocks, and I will sack him soon. My new house should have been completed by now. Brown-skinned girl, I am going to the tailor later this evening. Brown-skinned girl, I will take you to London one day'.

'Yes, sir, yes sir', I answer because that suddenly grabs my attention. 'Yes, sir. I will very much love to go to London. I come to attention, almost forgetting where I am. He lets out a wicked laugh, knowing he has my attention. And with that, he dismisses me with more Naira notes.

CHAPTER EIGHT

The years have gone by, signalled by the weird Christmas routines at the white house. Yes, that special day of the year when there is a lot of excitement and jubilation all around. That one day of the year when Mummy brings out her record player and positions it just outside the big sitting room on the side veranda with an LP titled *Collection of Christmas Carols* by Bing Crosby, which we play over and over, 'til dinner time. Soon I know how to sing 'The Twelve Days of Christmas', even in my sleep.

'Merry Christmas, Penelope'.

'Merry Christmas, Tolani', I reply myself as Penelope is in her own room; and I listen to the fireworks going off in the neighbourhood tucking myself into bed.

Birthday parties at school come and go. Our birthdays come and go without an acknowledgment from Mummy. Now I am a fully grown sixteen-year-old teenager, going on seventeen. On each birthday, I treat myself to extra portions of Mama Put rice and meat for my friends, and soft drinks of their choice, not letting on that it's my birthday. I keep this between Penelope and me, and I even treat Penelope and her friends to a celebration breakfast meal as well. And on each birthday, I wonder why Mama, my grandmother has not come to fetch me as she told me she would. The years have rolled by with no sign of Mama. I still do not know who my mother is, even though I now fully understand the meaning of the phrase 'bastard child'. I still cry to myself, but at this stage, crying is just an emotion that needs expressing and does not change my situation. But I still cry.

'Bride price' is the topic of today, our home economics teacher announces in class as we settle down for the lesson.

'Can anyone tell us what it means when a girl loses her virginity?' she asks.

Someone gives a long, convoluted answer.

'Thank you', she says, then reads from her notes. 'Traditionally, African societies lay great emphasis on virginity of women before marriage. To be a virgin bride is something to be proud of; a girl will command great respect from her prospective suitor and will attract a higher bride price. Among several repercussions for the loss of virginity before marriage are that girls will have to face social rejection, excommunication from family, and physical punishment. They will bring shame to their family if they lose their virginity before marriage'.

I can no longer listen. I feel like screaming, and I run out of the classroom. I feel so sick that I begin to retch and throw up uncontrollably. It dawns heavily on me what Chief has done to me and has continued to subject me to. How will I be able to tell Mama? What will I tell my prospective suitor when it comes time for fixing the bride price? Oh, my God! I need to go find Mama. I need to tell her before the time comes and I bring shame to the family. I start to hear voices in my head; the voices get louder, all talking at the same time, telling me to go find Mama, telling me to escape from the white house.

I must have sat in the grass hedge long after the closing bell. Penelope comes looking for me. I cannot control the 'uncharismatic' sessions; I am powerless to stop them. Still, the Naira notes continue to flow, but since that lesson, my mind has been so troubled as I find a way to go find Mama and tell her.

'Brown-skinned girl'. I lie there with Chief, listening to his usual idle chat, waiting for the Naira notes before I get dismissed. Bolts of lightning shoots through the drawn curtains followed by loud claps of thunder. The rainy season is here so not unusual of the Thunder and lighting.

'Hello, Dear', Mummy calls as she comes up the stairs. *Oh, my God!* How did we not hear the car drive up the gravel drive? Chief jumps off the bed. I have never seen such a big bulk of a man, as his belly has become larger and more rotund from regular meals of pounded yam and egusi soup. I move as fast as I can; he pushes me inside the en suite bathroom. I stand there quietly waiting for the calamity to befall me. Still standing in shock, Chief opens the bathroom door, now in his dressing gown, with Mummy standing beside him. He launches into a tirade of words: 'Dear, I have told you several times to make sure that there is enough water to flush down the toilet…. I won't have to call this stupid girl to fetch water and flush the toilet…'.

'You stupid girl!' Mummy joins in. 'C'mon, flush the toilet and get out of here before I give you a dirty slap'. I make a dash for my life, narrowly missing the back of her hand on my face.

In my bedroom, I swallow hard from the close shave. The voices in my head begin to laugh, and I join them in the laughter as well. Chief deserves an award for his performance, a golden cup award. I continue to laugh to myself as I hear Mummy trying to pacify him and calm his anger.

Not long after that close shave, I make a decision that will change things to come. I decide to start making entries in an old exercise book—diary entries, we are told they are called. I go back and enter every session from when it all started with Chief and every graphic detail. I become less attentive in school, unable to concentrate. My performance on tests drops, and the voices in my head don't stop. They tell me to run away from the white house, but where will I go? Do I confide in Honey? Will she let me go stay with her parents? Too many unanswered questions, but no one to offer any answers. And will Penelope understand and believe me if I tell her?

On the way to school, the voices are too troublesome, so I decide I cannot face school today.

'Penelope, you go ahead and catch the bus. I will see you in school', I say. I do not wait to see her reaction but cross to the other side of the road to catch the Danfo public transport going the opposite side of Ikoyi. 'Maroko! Maroko!' The bus pulls up, and I embark on the journey to Maroko. I have never been to Maroko before but hear about the beautiful people who live in the thriving fishing community by the banks of the river. Not that it makes any difference to me that morning; I just need to be elsewhere, away from school.

The Danfo reaches its destination by the banks of the river lined with canoes calling for passengers to go across. I look around. Maroko is too busy, and I may be spotted by a busybody who may just happen to know Mummy. I decide to travel with the canoe wherever the river flows. Holding up my skirt to keep it from getting wet, I clumsily board the unsteady canoe. I am the only passenger on board, not surprisingly, as commuters go the opposite way to whatever business of the day they have.

'Balance well', the man says, and we glide across the calmness of the river. I suddenly have a sense of freedom. When we come to a stop, I pay the man my fare and step onto a sandy beach of a little island, much in contrast to the murky banks of Maroko.

'Wetin dem call this place?' I ask the man in my near-perfect pidgin English the name of the place.

'Coconut Island'.

Ahhhhh, I do not need any further explanation. All along the shores of the beach are coconut trees with the palms swaying in the cool of the morning sun. It is almost like they are reaching to dip their tips in the gentle waves of the turquoise sea. I take off my rubber shoes and try to find some shade underneath a tree. The golden sand gives way softly under my feet. I immediately feel even more calm and relaxed, totally overtaken by the discovery of this beautiful island. And a funny thing—no voices in my head. Oh! What relief. I find a suitable spot and settle down, listening to the gentle waves and the gentle breeze rustling the palms of the coconut trees. I cast my eyes across the Atlantic, and in the far horizon, I see great ships, Ships bearing cargos of troubled human souls, chained down to unknown destinies with no escape, just stuck between the proverbial 'devil and the deep blue sea', being taken to the end of their rainbow—certainly a state of mind I am presently in.

My daydreaming is interrupted by the sudden excitement of a canoe rushing toward me. It's a fishing canoe, and I cannot help myself; I join the excitement of the rush, out of curiosity. The fishing boat has just landed with its early-morning catch. I peer inside and am amused at the sight of its stock. The market women begin haggling over their selection, almost bursting into quarrels with each other. I find this quite fascinating, and I think, *I will love to go fishing one day.* The excitement ends as quickly as it began, and people depart. I am now starting to get hungry, so I make my way farther inland and find a food seller. That is not unusual; where there is community, there will always be a Mama Put. After a plateful of rice, assorted meat, and Miranda soft drink, I make my way back to sit under my designated coconut tree.

I must have dozed off for a while, as I am nudged awake by this person.

'Hello'.

It is the voice of a white man. I quickly jump to my feet, realising how close to danger I am, trying to make a dash for it.

'No, please don't run. My name is Jeff'. He holds his hand out for a handshake. I look him over, cross that he interrupted my peace. He is well tanned with blond hair coming just to his shoulders, blue eyes, and chiselled facial structures, but with a very warm and friendly smile. Still I am not deceived by his looks.

'My name is T—' I stop short. 'My name is Tracey'. Mama taught me not to talk to strangers, but somehow this man, Jeff, does not look dangerous. 'Yes, my name is Tracey', I continue. 'I am waiting for my friend. She's just gone over there'. I point in any direction. 'And she will soon be back'.

'OK, then you don't mind if we wait for your friend together?'

'*We!*' This Jeff man is beginning to scare me now. I just want to be on my own. I need to think of how to shake him off, but he sits down and pulls me down to sit under the cool of the shade. 'Tell me to mind my own business, but dressed in your school uniform, isn't that where you should be at this time?'

'Yes, please mind your own business', I say with an irritation in my voice. Who is this stranger telling me where I should and should not be?

I just sit there silently, totally vexed with this stranger and wish he would pick himself up and be on his way. 'It appears your friend is not coming back for you', this man, Jeff, says after minutes of silence. He calls over the coconut seller to quench our thirst from the cool water. I decline; I do not feel comfortable sharing coconut juice with this stranger.

He goes into some conversation. I do not reply, and he goes on talking, just talking, but I do not care to listen, as my mind once again drifts across the Atlantic. I get another nudge. 'Tracey, you have not heard anything I have been saying', Jeff says.

'Oh! Is that the time?' I ask, glancing at the watch on his super-tanned wrist. 'Yes, it's time for me to go'. I stand up and shake the sand from my uniform. I take my leave and try to rush to catch the passenger canoe to Maroko. With a firm hand, Jeff holds my hand and pulls me toward him, stopping me in mid flight. Now we are standing face to face. 'Please, Tracey, I would like to see you again. I will be here, same time, same place, next week'.

I look at him weirdly.

'Please say you will come', he says.

'I...I don't know', I say, and I snatch my hand away from his, then proceed to board the canoe.

'I'll be waiting', he says as the canoe pulls away from the banks. During the entire journey back to the white house, I can't get this Mr Jeff out of my mind. A new feeling sweeps over me, and actually I really do want to see him again, to be in the warmth of those captivating, charming eyes. He seems friendly enough. I just may come back next week to see Mr Jeff.

Jeff is on my mind the whole rest of the week, and I may have just found a friend. But time will tell if I can share things with him, things that I am not able to share with Penelope, and not even Honey.

I make extra effort that morning, trying to look my best, rubbing Vaseline on my hair and combing it out, making it very high, fluffing it out so that it's bouncy. I make my way on the journey to Maroko and hope this extra attention to my dressing will not be a wasted effort if Jeff is not there. I do not have long to wait. I see Jeff walking calmly along the shores, letting the gentle waves lap at his legs. My heart skips a beat and begins to flutter. Shall I wait for him to come nearer, or do I go and jump in his arms? No, that will be too forward. I must maintain composure and not show my eagerness, as taught in *Pride and Prejudice*: 'If a woman is partial to a man, and does not endeavour to conceal it, he must find it out'. I smile to myself and wait for his approach.

Jeff and I meet a few more times at the beach, where I get to know he's twenty-four years old, an engineer, and works for an oil company. He is not married and lives in a flat on Victoria Island. I am beginning to like Jeff, and I think this feeling is called 'falling in love'! I have discovered falling in love, but at sixteen going on seventeen, can I wait to be older to fall in love with Jeff, now that love has found both Jeff and me?

CHAPTER NINE

The end-of-year examinations are approaching. I have performed badly on all my tests because of the distractions by Chief and the voices in my head. Only a miracle will help me not to fail. Failure means repeating a class and being held back. This is not good, very embarrassing, as the friends you have made all move ahead. The exam results are pasted by the staff room. I made it, and I got my miracle! I am not repeating the class. Huge relief. Huge, huge relief from the embarrassment and from the leathery hands of the koboko whip.

I am so happy, I need to share the good news, and I need to share it with someone special. I decide the next morning to go to the island. Coconut Island.

'Penelope, I will see you at school later', I say, and we part ways. I give her some money for Mama Put. She does not question where I go; she is now used to us parting and meeting up after school whenever I decide the order of the day.

I am not sure if Jeff will be here, as we have no prior arrangement, but I will give it a try. I sit and wait under the shade of the tree. The time ticks away, and no Jeff. I have almost given up when I see Jeff walking toward me. He is not alone but is next to a young female. I wait 'til they both stop by my tree.

'Hello, Tracey', he says, making his way toward me. I step back, filled with anger, jealousy, and sadness. *Who is this girl with Jeff?* I ask myself.

Quickly noticing my mood, Jeff says, 'Hey, meet Chi-Chi'.

I look the girl over, and she gives me the evil eyeball, standing with her arms akimbo, blowing bubbles, and chewing loudly on her bubble gum. Chi-Chi is much older than me, and I do not feel myself any match in my school uniform. I become immediately intimidated and look away from her evil eyes. Jeff pulls some Naira notes from his shorts, mumbles something, hands the notes to 'Chi-Chi', and dismisses her.

'Hey, Tracey', Jeff says, holding my hand, 'Chi-Chi' works the beach'.

'What do you mean, works the beach?'

'Chi--Chi is a prostitute, and I just use her company sometimes'.

I jerk my hand out of his in revulsion. Angry, but at what?

'Hey, Tracey—'

'I am not Tracey. My name's Tolani, and I am leaving now. Good-bye'. I am embarrassed that I lied about my name and angry at seeing Jeff with another girl.

He bursts out laughing. 'T'lani'.

'T-o-l-a-n-'. I spell it out for him slowly.

'T'lani', he repeats.

'OK, whatever'. I wonder what he finds so funny.

'OK', he says. 'Let's start all over again. My name is Jeff, Jeff Norfolk. Pleased to meet you, T'lani'.

'Pleased to make your acquaintance, Mr Jeff'.

I recite a passage from *Pride and Prejudice*, and we both burst into fits of childish laughter.

'You kept me waiting, T'lani. You did not come'.

'Well, I had to prepare for my exams, and I am glad to say I passed to the next class, which is what I have come to share with you'.

With that, he lifts me up, plants a cheeky kiss on my cheek, and says, 'Come, we must celebrate'.

We walk hand in hand, skipping along the shores, over the gentle waves of the turquoise sea.

We come to a beautiful white boat, and Jeff helps me on board.

'Well, come on board the *African Queen*', he says.

I gasp, taken aback by the size and beauty of this boat. It's like a house on water.

'I come to this island on the *African Queen* and sometimes go fishing on my days off', he says. 'Now, T'lani, I want to get to know you better. I can see there's a lot you are keeping back from me, but I like you. I really do like you and want to get to know you better'. He pours fruit juice for both of us.

I open my mouth to start talking but don't know where to start and quickly change the subject. 'This is a beautiful boat. Will you take me fishing someday?' I am already deciding I will be seeing a lot more of Jeff, to keep him from ever getting back with Chi-Chi.

'Yes, it will be my pleasure', he replies.

I sip the juice and feel the slow bobbing of the *African Queen* on the Atlantic. Jeff soon breaks the long silence by cosying up next to me, putting his arms around me. I do not resist, and I stay there in the comfort of his arms, watching the clouds float by. Gently, Jeff lifts my head up to his and places his lips over mine, taking full control of my senses. I yield to his touch, to this long, lingering full-on kiss. A warm feeling completely overtakes me—not like the drunkenness of the palm wine, but excitedly warm feelings all over me. Butterflies gently flutter in my tummy. Yes, I am truly in love, in love with Jeff, Slowly I pull away.

'I have to go now, Jeff. I don't want to miss the canoe'.

'T'lani, I would like to see more of you and want you to come visit me at home on Victoria Island'.

'I can't promise anything, but will try', I reply.

He gives me his address, which I memorise. And with another lingering kiss, Jeff helps me off the *African Queen* and walks me to catch the canoe back to reality.

Penelope is waiting at the bus stop earlier than usual; I have often had to do the waiting.

'Tolani, there is trouble', she says. 'Our principal gave me this letter to give to Mummy. I think you have to see it first'. She brings out the letter from her bag. It reads as follows:

Dear Madam,

It has been brought to my attention that Tolani has not been attending classes regularly, and her form teachers are concerned. I need to have a meeting with you to discuss this matter and see how we can support Tolani to ensure that she keeps up to her best performance.
Yours faithfully,
Principal

I become overtaken by sudden fury and anger, tear the letter into shreds, and throw into the flowing gutter. I grab Penelope by the collar, and with the same fury in my eyes, I speak to her in a guttural voice, as if taken over by Beelzebub himself, 'If you ever tell Mummy of this letter, you are dead! Do you understand me?'

She looks shocked and nods her head in fright. With that, we make our way home, me with a spring in my step. I am in love, and nothing will spoil that for me.

━┿━ ┿━

I plan my meetings with Jeff more carefully and space them out so my attendance at school is not so obvious, though school is not busy after exams. I decide I need to see Jeff before we break for the long holiday; I need a master plan, a fool proof master plan to be away for the weekend. What will I tell Mummy? I have no Plan B, so Plan A has to work!

'Good afternoon, Ma'. We greet Mummy in the big sitting room. No acknowledgment—not that we expect any. 'Please, Ma, our teacher has organised a school excursion for the students who study French to visit Togo'.

Sure, that's where Monsieur Garcon comes from, I think.

'I have been selected, and we leave on the school bus after school this Friday and are coming back on Sunday'.

I do not stop to breathe, as I need to make it convincing. Deep breath out! Mummy gives no reaction but dismisses me with a wave of her hand.

'Thank you, Ma'.

God! What have I just done? I think as I enter my bedroom. *I have just gone and dug my own grave and will soon be buried by Mummy.* After the evening chores, Mummy indicates to me by saying, 'You' and asks how much will it cost.

'No money, Ma'. Our teacher says the school has paid for the cost'.

She hands me a 20-Naira note for food.

'Thank you, Ma'.

I cannot wait for Friday morning. I board a taxi and head for Victoria Island, to Jeff's house.

'Sanu Megidah'. I greet the gateman.

'Owka no dey, wait I call am for steward' the gateman explains that Jeff is not in but that I should wait whilst he gets the Steward.

I do not need much of an explanation to be let in by the steward, and I wonder about the ease with which I have been let in. Is this the norm for girls to come visiting Jeff, and is it nothing new? I banish the jealous thought. *I shall not ruin this weekend, this rare opportunity that may never come by again.* In Jeff's flat, my inquisitiveness takes me 'round the house, and I notice that the walls are adorned with pictures, hand paintings, unfinished sketches, and African carvings. The occupant of this house has really fallen in love with everything Africa.

I make myself comfortable and cosy on the settee and get waited on by the steward, who makes sure to extend Oga Jeff's hospitality to his waiting guest. I must have fallen asleep. I am gently woken by a warm kiss on my lips. 'Hello, T'lani. What a pleasant surprise!'

His enchanting eyes cannot hide the surprise in his smile, and I smile back. 'Hello, Jeff'.

'Godfrey! Dinner for two, please'.

At dinner, I notice that Jeff is not eating much and sits staring most of the time.

'My grandmother tells me it's rude to stare, Mr Jeff Norfolk'.

'Sorry, can't help myself. You look even more beautiful than when we first met, T'lani. 'Come. Come pose for me'.

I look at him, confused.

'Yes, I have to paint this beautiful angel'. He proceeds to position me.

'Wait a minute', I say. I whip out my comb and give my Afro a good combing. 'Now I am ready, Mr Jeff!'

Jeff's production of the sketch is so beautiful, though it's long from being finished. When this is finished, it will sit on my office desk Jeff says to me proudly.

He turns on the stereo and shows me some moves. For a white man, he does have some cool moves. I try the only moves I know, the JB moves. The lights are dim, the music changes from the Jackson Five to Marvin Gaye, and slowly Jeff pulls me closer to this chest. We dance to the slow rhythm of 'Let's Get It On', melting into each other's arms, our souls entwined, kneeling onto the soft rug as our bodies become one. This ebony and ivory are becoming one, locked in a slow, passionate kiss. Slowly he unbuttons my blouse. My nipples rise to the soft touch of his palms. My body is completely overtaken by the loving of Jeff, Jeff Norfolk, and as his hand goes farther into my skirt, I suddenly stop him short.

'No! No! You must stop'.

I push him off of me. 'I am sorry. I…I…can't. I just can't. I am not what or who you think I am. Jeff', I continue to plead, 'I have been deflowered'.

He knows there is something really serious, and he leans back against the sofa. 'Do you want to tell me about it?'

I tell Jeff all about it, all about Chief.

'I am sorry, T'lani. I am sorry. I promise you, I will make it end'. He cups my face in his hands, wiping away the tears that are flowing. 'Ssssh…sssssh…'. He holds my head to his chest, and I let the tears flow freely onto his warm body. Certainly, no one's getting it on for the rest of the evening.

'C'mon, T'Lani, I know what might just cheer you up. We are going out', Jeff says.

'I am not really feeling up to it, Jeff'.

But why not? I freshen up, and Jeff gives me one of his silk shirts, a pink silk shirt that just seems to caress my whole body. It flows to my mid thighs, like mini dress, and we head out. After several minutes of driving, we arrive on a very busy and narrow street. The buzz for the night time is rather interesting and different from the quiet quarters of Ikoyi and Victoria Island. Jeff manages to find a parking space, and we alight. I hold on tightly to Jeff's arm, feeling rather uncomfortable at the looks we are getting because I am a black girl in the arms of a white man. 'Prostitute' comes to mind, but I do not care. Outside this building with the sign 'Africa 70-Kalakuta Republic Nightclub', Jeff pays the entry fee. Inside this dark venue with the aroma of funny-smelling cigarettes, the air is filled with loud instrumental music. It's a nightclub. Jeff feels my discomfort as we try to find somewhere to sit.

'Jeff, I really do not feel comfortable here. Please, can we go?'

We get up, and I am still holding on tightly to Jeff. We go to a corner, and Jeff produces a funny-looking cigarette. The puzzled look on my face says it all. Trying to make my voice heard, I say, 'I did not know that you smoke, Jeff'.

He gives me a smile, lights the funny-looking cigarette, takes a long pull, and says, 'Here, try it'.

'No'. I push his hand away.

'Try it, 'T'lani'. He places it on my lips. I take a drag—cough, cough, splutter, splutter—and try to keep myself from choking.

Jeff pats my back. 'Here, try again. This time, take a long, slow pull, hold it in, and exhale. How does that feel?'

'Don't know', I say with a shrug.

'What is it called, anyway?'

'It's herbal. Another try?'

I take several more pulls of this 'herbal', now feeling the buzz of the atmosphere.

The music tempo increases, announcing the entry of Fela and the dancing girls and more excitement on the floor. This night, Jeff and I both gyrate to the rhythms of the drums of the Afrobeat. The distinctive beat of the African Gbedu drums takes me to a high level of spirituality that seems to connect me to my inner self.

CHAPTER TEN

'Good morning, Sweetheart', Jeff says.

I stretch, yawn, and ask, 'What time is it?'

'Time to get up and have a shower. I have a surprise for you'.

After a nice, warm shower, Jeff hands me the most beautiful green bikini swimsuit I have ever seen. It's new; the price tag is still on it.

'How did you guess my size?'

'Easy. Only one size fits a beautiful body like yours'. Jeff gives me another one of his freshly ironed silk shirts as an over shirt, as we are going out. 'It's a surprise', he tells me.

Driving along in his luxurious Range Rover throws a new perspective on travel, and things seem even more beautiful. We arrive at the jetty where the *African Queen* is moored. I clumsily try to get on board but nearly fall into to the Atlantic Ocean, so Jeff helps me aboard.

'And where are we going?' I ask.

'Going fishing'.

I clap my hands together with glee like an excited young child.

'Oh, Jeff! I have always wanted to go fishing. I love you!'

'I love you more, T'lani. Hold on tight', he says as the engine comes to life.

'Yes, Captain Jeff!' I throw him a mock salute. We pull anchor, and Jeff proceeds to teach me how to bait hooks and throw lines. Such a wonderful experience! I manage to catch little fish, which Jeff unhooks and throws back into the ocean.

'These we don't eat, but leave for another day'.

We sail a bit farther and come to a small island—not Coconut Island. It seems to never stop. It fascinates me how the Atlantic is dotted with small, beautiful, unexplored islands. We disembark. Godfrey has prepared a picnic basket, and I help Jeff lay out the spread on the picnic blanket. The selection of delicacies makes my saliva perform acrobatics on my tongue. The day has been so exciting so far, and I just wish it will not come to an end.

Jeff and I lie on our backs and watch the clouds gently float by. 'You see that one there?'

'Yes'.

'That is me, you, and our children'.

I laugh. 'Oh, Jeff, you're so funny. But perhaps if you wish hard enough, your wishes might just come true'. I know inside, though, that is highly unlikely to happen.

We talk about school things and non-school things. 'T'lani, I want to marry you', he says. He rolls over on his side. *Is this what's called a proposal?*

'I want you to be the mother of my children'. He looks serious and is not waiting for me to respond. He seals my lips with a warm, lingering kiss, his hands slowly caressing my body, going all the way this time. 'Wait a minute', he whispers and pulls out condoms. 'We can't make babies yet, not just yet'. And Jeff makes slow love to me on this beautiful island, the Isle of T'lani.

Sunday morning fills me with much trepidation and anxiety because the weekend is coming to an end, and I wonder what lies ahead at the white house. Jeff insists on dropping me back at home. We get to the closest bus stop, and he attempts to give me kiss. I am holding back tears.

'When will I see you again, T'lani?'

'I don't know', I reply, shrugging my shoulders. With that, I make my way to the white house.

The last few days of school, lessons are over, and reports have been handed out. I do not feel like what I see as just wasting time at school. I feel the need for some quiet time, away from 'friends for food', away from Honey, and not in the company of Penelope.

'Penelope! See you after school. Make sure you wait for me at the bus stop', I say, and we part ways. Surprisingly, Penelope has never asked where I go. I take the bus to Maroko. I need to be on Coconut Island before the long holiday.

I sit there under the palms of the tree, not thinking of anything, just sitting and listening to the gentle lapping of the waves of the turquoise sea. It is as if it is washing away the past and revealing new beginnings. Time to go. Good-bye, island. I journey to meet up with Penelope at the bus stop.

Back from last day of school and fearful of what the long holiday will bring, Penelope and I make our way to the white house.

'Good afternoon, Ma'.

'You'. Mummy motions to me. 'Come, stand there'.

It's not looking good; I sense a bad omen in the room. I stand there for what seems like an eternity, and there it is, right in Mummy's hands—an exercise book. My exercise book! The one in which I chronicled all of my secrets about Chief. Mummy opens it slowly and reads through the first page. Halfway through, she leaps to her feet and grabs the leather whip. It comes hard down and fast, each flailing arm of the leather whip tearing away at my raw flesh, my face, my arms, all over my body. I plead for Mummy to stop. I plead for my life, but she continues with increased strength, with anger in her voice. 'You will die today'.

I feel the walls closing in on me. I cannot breathe. Darkness overcomes me, and my legs slowly give way from under me....

CHAPTER ELEVEN

I try to open my eyes. It hurts. I hurt all over. My body is racked with pain all over. I open my eyes halfway, blinded by the bright lights. I think I have died and gone to heaven, as I've heard that in heaven, the lights are very bright. I manage to speak from the soreness of my throat. 'Where am I?' I whisper.

'Ssshh, you are all right', the voice says.

A figure comes over, dressed all in white. Yes; for sure I am in heaven. 'I am Nurse Titi, and you are going to be fine'.

I soon fall into a deep sleep.

When I finally wake up, I realise I am in hospital, my whole body heavy with bandages. My head hurts the most. 'What happened to me?'

'Don't worry about that. You just get better', the nurse says.

As the days go by, I begin to regain my strength and begin to ask more questions from Nurse Titi, as she seems to be the nicest of the nurses. But she will not yield any answers. She helps me to the bathroom, and I stand in front of the mirror. My face is all swollen, and my head is heavily bandaged. I run my hand over my face; it looks like I have been in a couple of rounds with that boxer, Muhammad Ali. I do not cry; I have no more tears to shed. The voices tell me not to cry, not to cry....

'Nurse Titi', I say to her one morning after a cocktail of pills. 'Please, I need you to help me. I need you to help me contact Jeff. I tell her all about him. The way she looks at me, it's as if she thinks I may be suffering from delusions. She does not believe me and increases the dosage of the sedatives. 'Please, Nurse Titi. I am not mad. You must help me get in touch with Jeff or let me go and look for him. And please don't give me any more of those injections; they make me sleep for too long. I need to be awake just in case Mama comes, in case Chief comes to see me'.

She takes a long and worried look at me. 'OK, OK, Mrs Jeff', she says. But Nurse Titi is not moved; she is convinced that I have lost my marbles. I give up asking her or even talking to her about Jeff, but I can see that she has been placed there specifically to keep an eye over me. I try to focus on getting better and stronger, as I am now determined that once out of the hospital, I am not going back to the white house. Anywhere but the white house.

The head bandage comes off, revealing ugly-looking, rough stitches going from one side of my face to the other. How can I carry this around? Will Jeff recognise me? Will I recognise myself? Will Mama recognise me? The recollections of what happened on that day come flooding back, and now I cannot hold myself back from crying. I sob my heart out. I am truly broken! No one visits, not Penelope, not Mama.

'Good morning, Tolani. You are going home. You are being discharged'.

I show no emotions. What is Nurse Titi expecting? Some sort of celebratory dance? 'Your sister has come to take you home'.

With that, Penelope peers around the door. I can see the shock on her face, and she is speechless. She stops eating the half-eaten bread in her hand. I give her a wry smile.

'Hello, Penelope'.

I think someday this girl will die of gluttony. She is always eating—always, even if the sky is falling, Penelope will always be eating.

'Thank you, Nurse Titi. Good-bye, Nurse Titi'.

On the bus Journey home, I pray that some calamity will befall me in some accident and will finish up what Mummy and the leather whip did not achieve. I pray that my skull will crack open and smash into bits like Mummy's broken dish the very first day Chief laid his filthy hands on my person.

'Tolani', Penelope says between mouthfuls of bread and akara, fried bean dough. 'I have something to tell you'.

'What?' I ask quietly, still trying to adjust to the busy streets, the noise, after a long spell in the protective environment of the hospital.

'Mama is dead!'

'What do you mean, Mama is dead, and who told you Mama is dead, and which Mama?'

I throw her a barrage of questions to make sure she knows what she's saying.

'Mama, your grandmother, is dead'. Penelope looks serious, and now I am convinced she is telling the truth, as I tell her a lot about Mama, so she knows about Mama.

'She died a few days after you were taken to hospital, and I overheard Mummy talking on the phone about funeral arrangements and plans. She was actually buried last week'.

I hold my head in my hands. *Oh, no, please! It's not true. Please tell me it's not true. Mama can't die. Mama can't die....*

Penelope puts her arms around me. 'Tolani, you must stop crying before we get home'.

I do not see Mummy; Penelope brings me breakfast and evening meals. Each morning, I hear the key to my room turn, locking me inside the room all day. 'Hello, dear. Yes, dear'. I hear the usual greetings of Mummy and Chief in the adjoining room. So Chief is very much around. Surely he must have heard of what happened to me, and if so, why has he not asked about me? Where have all his promises of taking me to London gone? I am resigned to spending the rest of the holidays as a prisoner in this room, to be fed and watered by Penelope and allowed out only for showers. Still I do not see Mummy.

Relief comes when the holiday is over and the new school term starts. For the first time in more than eight weeks, I see Mummy. 'Good Morning, Ma'.

No response. I bid good-bye to Penelope at the bus stop as I part ways with her and wave down a taxi to Victoria Island.

CHAPTER TWELVE

'Good morning, Meghidah!' I greet Malam gateman at Jeff's flat.

'Ah! Good morning, sister. Owka Jeff e no dey', he answers that Jeff is not in.

'Wait! I come'. 'Come here, Meghidah!' I raise my voice. 'What do you mean, Owka Jeff? No dey? Open the gate now, now!'

I begin to lose my temper at the effrontery of the gateman keeping me outside the gate.

'Owka Jeff say make I giff you this', he says, handing me a white envelope. I snatch it from him, eyeing him suspiciously, and open the envelope addressed to T'lani.

Dearest Sweet-at-heart:

Sorry at what you are feeling right now as you read this letter. Did not know where to come looking for you.

Have had to travel to Scotland to manage an urgent project and will be away for a couple of months. Darling, I am really sorry for not being able to tell you before travelling.

Babe, you must write to me at my parents' address:
3 The Elms
Primrose Hill
London
N1 3LU

Missing you already, promise you will write.

Love always,
Jeff

I let out a deafening scream, wailing loudly. I squeeze the letter up in my hands. The voices are screaming louder than my wails, and I cry uncontrollably, each violent sob accompanied by the loud screams in my head. I feel a hand gently helping me sit on a bench. I continue to cry for help, for the voices to stop, and I cry 'til my head begins to ache.

I slowly regain composure of my senses, straighten myself, and take the first Danfo bus to nowhere, in search of calmness from the voices. This time I wait for Penelope outside the school gate, and we travel home together, not exchanging one word.

Just before the evening chores start, I make my way to my room, close the door behind me, and for the first time ever, pull open the French double doors to reveal the balcony, letting in the warm afternoon breeze.

With that, I hike up my skirt, climb onto the balcony ledge overlooking the banana grove and pineapple grove, and with a push, I lunge forward, let myself go, along with my unborn child....

CHAPTER THIRTEEN

I hover above the men and women in white clothing and watch their frantic efforts to tend to this body lying on the hospital bed. This small, fragile body with tubes coming from my face, oxygen pumping to my chest, wires plugged into all sorts of machines. I hover closely to see the body of Tolani lying below. One, two, three, bzzzzzz… comes from the defibrillator pump. Pump, pump, pump, to the count of three. Stand back: bzzzzzzzz.

'Doctor, no sign'.

'No, don't give up on her. Let's try again. Keep trying. Stand back'.

Bzzzzzzzzz. A sudden jolt of electricity. Whooosh. Beep, beep, beep. The machine slowly comes to life, and I hear sighs of relief all around me. 'We got life. She's back! We have a pulse. Her heart is beating'.

The machine continues with a slow and steady rhythm.

'Congratulations, team! Well done. Sadly, she lost the baby'.

The room becomes quiet, and I continue to hear the steady rhythm of the machine. I cannot move or open my eyes. I want to cry. 'Baby, I lost a baby…'. I drift off.

Slowly I open my eyes and look around the familiar, not-so-far-in-the-distance surroundings of the hospital. I try to get up but am unable to move with wires and tubes still attached to my body. Seeing that I am struggling, a nurse comes to my bedside and helps me onto a bedpan.

I try to move my legs, but they are swollen, pain-ful, bruised. I become scared. My body hurts all over. Panic takes over me, and I let out a loud scream. 'Why did the doctors save me? Why did they save me? Please let me die. Let me die!' I beg the nurse, 'Nurse, please, you must let me die'. I sob, then feel a sharp prick of the needle and drift off to sleep.

I try to suppress everything that led to me to be-ing in the hospital. I supress Jeff but remember the last moment before the fall. Dr Majekodunmi, with a kind-looking face, on the morning rounds with his team, says, 'Young lady, what pushed you to take such action?'

I look at him and think, *Pushed, pushed by the voices, pushed by life at the white house.*

'You are very lucky to be alive, with only minor bruises and a dislocated ankle and shoulder'.

He rattles off some other medical jargon that is not clear to me, then says, 'We will put a plaster cast on the ankle and shoulder and keep you in hospital so that we can continue to monitor you'.

Hold on. I think you have failed to mention how frantic efforts were made to save my life, failed to mention the aborted/miscarried foetus. I let out a long, drawn-out sigh.

With just half use of my faculties, I get moved from the intensive care unit and am able to hobble around with the aid of crutches. I become a long-term resident of the unit. Visitors come and go, but there are no visitors for me. No Penelope, no one. Some days are better than others. I feel like sleeping the whole day or pretend to sleep and overhear the visitors who have come to visit their loved ones. They whisper, 'Does this young girl have family? Maybe she is an orphan'. I suppress the voices, suppress Jeff from my thoughts, banish Chief from my thoughts. *Tolani, get a hold of yourself,* I think. *Otherwise, the injection jab will come.* I'll bet the nurses enjoy the indiscriminate use of the injection that immediately does what it is meant for: to keep me quiet.

On very good days, I sit at the nurses' station and listen to gossip about which doctor is having an affair with whom, who fancies which nurse, and which affair has just collapsed…. Still no visitors.

The plaster cast is coming off today, the nurse tells me, and I pretend to be delighted at the news. The bones have healed very well. Dr Majekodunmi pulls and stretches my freshly revealed ankle and arm. 'Any pain there? Here? What about here?'

'No, no, and no', I answer.

'But we have to keep you in hospital for further physiotherapy to make sure everything is fine. We also want to keep an eye on you'.

'Thank you, doctor'.

Physio means the nurses have to ensure that I walk around the wards more often. During the ambulating sessions, I am nosy about every patient's business. The hospital wards have now become my home, but for how long? The question is not far from being answered as I get a visitor one afternoon, and she is led to my bedside. 'My name is François. Madam has asked me to come and take you home, and I will be looking after you from now on. From the tone of her English, I detect a French accent. I ask in French,

'Etes-vous ma gardienne', 'are you my care giver?

'Oui'. She looks surprised.

'Parlez-vousFrancais

'Justeen peu', Just a little I replied.

With that established, François and I build a bond that will see me through these troubled times.

And with my crutches, I bid my farewell to the nurses and hold onto François for support. Mummy has afforded us the luxury of travelling in a chartered taxi home. François keeps talking on the way. I shut my eyes and wish she would just shut up as I prepare my mind for not knowing what to expect.

Oh, no! We do not go home to the white house but to an even bigger white house, a newly constructed 'bigger white house'. So it's true what Chief said about this construction.

'Banish Chief from your mind', I hear the voices in my head say.

François takes me around the house over the gravel drive right to the back of the property, to the boys' quarters, where I have been given a room to share with her. In the room are my single bed, a table, a desk, and a bare cement floor. I sit on the bed and take a long look at the room, then let out a deep sigh. François lays out the bottles of pills I have been given to take daily. Big white ones for pain, little blue ones for sleeping, 'and yellow ones for when you hear voices', she tells me. Then, with a look of concern on her face, she says to me,

'Bienvenue a la Maison', welcoming me home.

'Merci', I reply.

I must have fallen asleep, as I am woken up by the voices of both Chief and Mummy in the morning, telling off the gardener for failing to trim back the bougainvillea and letting the hibiscus plant wither. I shut my eyes. *Welcome home, Tolani.*

I have not seen Mummy or Penelope since I came back, but with the bond I have established with François, I begin to trust her and ask about Penelope. She says she has seen her but is unable to tell me anything about her. I actually believe that Mummy must have some kindness deep down in her heart, which is yet to be revealed. She makes sure I do not starve and has given me shelter, which I am grateful for. François is given a weekly allowance for all my needs. I control how she spends it, and I save the change.

Now that I am able to put more support on my ankle and use the crutches less, I go to the market with François—just any excuse to be out of the house will do. When I am not out and about with François, I sit outside my room, listening to the steward's transistor radio. Inflation, inflation, inflation. Food scarcity. 'Operation Feed the Nation' is all I hear about. *'Nah wah O!'* I exclaim to myself concerned on the state of Nigeria's economy which is plummeting fast. Momentarily, I stare at the pineapple and banana groves, which have grown. Chief must really love his pineapples and bananas, though I can swear that at the old white house, I never saw him or Mummy eat them. They were always given out to guests and whoever cared to have them.

On this sunny afternoon, gazing at the grove, Chief comes for his regular afternoon stroll, as I have heard him do. François asks that I go inside because Chief must not see me.

'Why?' I ask.

'Madam's orders'.

I look at her with fire blazing from my eyes and say, 'Leave me be. I am not moving from here!'

As Chief approaches, I remain unmoved. He takes a glance at me, looks away, and continues on his stroll. At that moment, I decide that nothing is ever going to hold me back. *What did not kill me has made me stronger,* I say to myself, and I let out a loud laugh. François looks at me with that worried look still on her face, and she gives me the 'when you hear voices' pills.

CHAPTER FOURTEEN

I hear a soft tap, tap on the door early one morning, and François rises from her mat to see who it is. She lets Penelope in, and I rise, still groggy from the sleeping tablets. Penelope looks happy to see me. She explains that Mummy has forbidden her to come and see me, and she must not be seen talking to me. She must quickly go, as she will get into big trouble if Mummy ever finds out.

'Wait', I say. 'Please give the steward all my school books to bring for me'.

'OK', she whispers, and she departs as quietly as she came. *Poor Penelope*, I think. *It must be really sad and lonely for her in there.*

Having secured my books, I throw myself back into my studies. I have missed almost a year, and I know that I will not be able to sit for the WAEC board exams (West African Examinations), as my class has just completed them. Without a school certificate, the future seems rather bleak. With the help of François, I make enquires at the secondary school, and with the savings from my weekly allowance, I enrol in evening classes for extra tutorial support for students who have missed the opportunity to get good grades at the first sitting.

I become frustrated at having to wait another long year or for the start of the evening sessions. François becomes even more concerned at seeing my troubled mind. She says to me one morning. 'Tolani, I know of a pastor, a powerful man of God, who will pray for you and make all these troubled voices stop'.

'Please leave me be, François, leave me be!' I say in a very stern voice, but she refuses to shut up as she hands me the 'when you hear voices' pills.

'I promise you...', she says, then breaks into French lingo. She is getting rather angry at me and gives me a lecture about getting healed and all that stuff.

'OK, OK. Take me to your wonderful pastor man', I say in the most sarcastic tone of voice.

Powerful Pastor Man of God does not live in a church building but some shack in Bar Beach, I discover as we make our way through the various shacks to locate the Man of God. As crude as the ramshackle shack looks, it is lit up with candles of various colours, shapes, and sizes, and incense fills the air. Powerful Man of God, in a familiar white robe with dreadlocks, looks rather unkempt for a holy person. He gets into a trance and begins to chant and hop about in the most comical way. I hold myself back from laughing. He comes out of the trance as quickly as he had started and tells me what my programme will be. I am to embark on a programme of praying and fasting, fasting and praying, for seven days, and I have to stay at the beach for the whole seven-day programme. I look at François. She agrees to the programme on my behalf without asking me first, so my healing has been decided for me by François and the Prophet Man of God.

A white gown is quickly produced to my specification, and I am robed in white. Both François and I are to spend the next seven days here, with no one knowing my whereabouts. Not that I will be missed at the 'even bigger white house', but if anything should go wrong…. I just have to trust François.

Daytime is a series of purging baths to stop the 'hearing voices of demons' of several kinds with holy water. I drink holy water, too, and in the evening after each tiresome session, I sit at the edge of the beach watching the now-calm waters and gentle waves lapping at the shores. It's so interesting how the beach comes alive at sundown and takes on a totally new perspective from daytime. It begins to fill up with expatriates. I take a long stroll along the shoreline and watch with keen interest how the girls 'work the beach'. They never seem to be short of clients.

The week is over, and I have one final holy-water bath. Honestly, in some funny sort of way, I feel quite relaxed and relieved, which I put down to just being in a different environment with a fresh sea breeze, away from the 'even bigger white house'. That is what the doctor should have prescribed instead of the cocktail of medications.

And with the renewed energy, I am now able to concentrate more on my studies. The examination dates are fast approaching, so I have to give it my best shot; there are no excuses.

'Tolani', François says after breakfast.

'Yes, François?'

'Madam says that my work here is completed, and I will be leaving'.

'When do you leave?' I ask.

'This Friday'.

'And where will you be going?'

'I will be returning back home to Togo and set up a small business'.

I let out a big sigh, say nothing, and resume my studies. Of course I will miss François; she has grown to be like a big sister to me. But now the bond must be severed—no more emotional ties. My last paper is due in two days, and any emotions will destroy what both

François and I have worked hard to achieve. I will deal with this sad news later.

On Friday morning, as I am preparing for my last paper, I can see François beginning to tidy up and pack her few belongings. The room begins to empty, and she approaches to give me a good-bye hug. I put my hands out to stop her and say,

'Adieu, François'.

Adieu, mon cher Le Tolani'.

And with that, I head to the centre to take my last exam. My weekly allowance continues; Mummy sends it to me through the steward.

CHAPTER FIFTEEN

There is a while yet before I will get the result of my WAEC exams and Weeks of just idling about becomes too frustrating, so I decide to 'work the beach'. I can no longer continue to sit alone in this room and depend on the allowance from Mummy. I take the decision to become a prostitute.

My first client approaches me on the beach, and I ask, 'Oga' a term used in describing boss, you get protection?' Mama will be turning in her grave to see me like this.

On a good weekend, I make between 500 and 800 Naira, much of it from expatriate customers. Baba Gateman is beginning to question my movements as I come back in the early hours of the morning. To buy his silence, I give him regular tips and buy my free pass to the house. With my weekly allowance, savings, and these new earnings, I open a savings account at the Union Bank and watch my savings grow each week.

The results are out today, and I set out early to avoid the rush of students. A queue has already formed by the time I arrive. I find my exam number and run my finger along…C,C,C, six credits. I have passed all my subjects with credits. Well done, Tolani Pearce, well done! I congratulate myself and head to the nursing school with my results to register for a two-year diploma in nursing. I pay all the fees, as well as accommodation fees for the hostel. The excitement, the jubilation! But there is no one to share it with. I visit Coconut Island, sit quietly under the cool of the shade, and listen to the gentle lapping of the waves. It is quite dark by the time I arrive, and this time, Baba Gateman refuses me entry. 'Madam say make I no open gate for you'.

I beg Baba Gateman, 'Just allow me for this night. See, as mosquito, dey bite me. Please, I beg'.

He remains unmoved.

'OK, take this'. I thrust into his palm a 50-Naira note, and he opens the gate quietly. It's amazing what a 50 note can do. It buys an everlasting silence.

I get up before daybreak and gather what belongings I have; they all fit into my old school bag. I shut the door behind me. Then I make my way to the pineapple and banana groves. With all the strength in my body, I pull down every banana tree and pull up every pineapple head. The ones that refuse to budge, I stamp the life out of them. I dust off my hands. Ahhh, how nice that feels.

I soon settle into lectures at the nursing school and hostel life, too. I watch how the girls gather every evening waiting to catch a boyfriend or two. With no particular intention in mind, this evening I decide to hang out with a student nurse who is waiting for her boyfriend. A big car pulls up, and the driver approaches me, saying that his Oga 'Big Man' wants to see me. The window is rolled down as I reach the car. 'Hello, Baby. Jump in. Let Big Daddy wine and dine you', this big man says in a strong Igbo accent.

Well, I think. *I've got nothing to lose*, and the driver opens the door to let me in.

I watch 'Big Daddy' dive into the assortment of Chinese dishes, from won-ton to poo-poo platter, and amuse myself with his table manners, or shall I say lack of etiquette. I throw him wry smiles from across the table. I push my fried rice around and take little sips of the Chapman drink. I strategize in my head how I am going to straddle this big man later on tonight when he asks for sex.

Nooo, Big Daddy does not want sex; he wants me to dance. 'Baby, come, dance for Big Daddy. Show Big Daddy some moves', he says when we arrive at his house. What relief, and I actually begin to enjoy the evening as Big Daddy and I share something in common—yes, the love of Fela music. And yes, I dance. I do African dance, fire dance, and even' Lady' dance.

'Oh, Baby, you're sooo good. Come give Big Daddy a kiss'.

Mwah! Mwhah! I plant two pecks on his cheeks as he spreads out on the sofa.

'Big Daddy has a gift for you', he says. He pulls open a concealed drawer under the table where he lines up the 'white stuff'. Among the notes of money, I catch a glimpse of a handgun, and I temporarily freeze. He hands me a wad of notes. 'Oh, Baby, treat yourself'.

'Bulldog, Bulldog', he calls to his driver. 'Come, take my baby home'.

As I make a fast exit, I hear him say, 'See you next week. Same time, same place'.

The following morning before lectures, I make my way to Bristol Hotel to the black marketplace to exchange the dollars Big Daddy gave me. I hand over the wad of the dollar notes, and the mallam; the foreign currency changer holds each one up against the light. I hold my breath, hoping they are not fake. I have often heard of girls being paid fake notes when I was working the beach. He brings out his calculator and shows me the sum: 2,500 Naira. What! He seems to take forever counting and recounting, but then he hands me the Naira in exchange, all 2,500, talking of striking it lucky the first time. I think I may have just bagged myself a sugar daddy. I deposit this in my savings account. Big Daddy 'sugar daddy' never fails to deliver—more dollars and jewellery, my first diamond bracelet. 'Do you like it? It's all the way from Dubai'.

'Yes, Big Daddy, it's gorgeous. Thank you'. Mwah! Mwah!

When Big Daddy goes to visit his family in Enugu or on business or takes trips to Dubai or America, I hang out with Dr Kunle, my boyfriend. Well, every girl must have a boyfriend; they are like an accessory that every girl must have. He is tall and handsome, and he worships the ground I walk on, but he is not my type. Dr Kunle wants marriage. 'Tolani', he says, 'please come and meet my parents. I really want to marry you, and my parents want to meet you'.

'Don't worry, Kunle. Once I graduate, I will come and meet your parents, and we can talk marriage'.

'Promise', he says.

'I promise', I say while doing the crossing of the fingers thing behind my back.

Kunle enjoys jazz music, and we visit the newly opened jazz club. Kunle does not like the music of Fela, but I make him take me to Kalakuta Shrine all the same. There is a look of shock and horror on his face the first time I light up the herbal joint and have a looong pull. I connect with my inner self and hone my dance steps for the private audience composed of Big Daddy.

CHAPTER SIXTEEN

The years have gone by really quickly, and the final year is coming to a close with preparations for the finals. 'Tolani Pearce', the lecturer announces at the end of the session, 'report to the principal's office'. That sounds ominous. Reporting to the principal's office means one of two things: underperformance or non -payment of school fees. Neither applies to me. So with much trepidation, I join the queue with some other students the principal has summoned.

'Good afternoon, sir'.

I get invited to sit down, and the principal hands me a brown envelope, which I open with shaking hands. 'Congratulations on the award of your scholarship', he says.

'Thank you, sir! Thank you, sir!' I can't quite take it all in until I get outside and read the whole contents of the letter and documents over and over, from top to bottom. Among the students who were nominated for the scholarship, I am one of the few successful ones.

I have been awarded a nursing scholarship to further my studies in the United Kingdom with bursary—accommodations and all expenses paid—and I will fly out after graduation. I do something I have not done in a very long time: I fall to my knees and thank the Good Lord in the Heavens above. Tears of joy begin fill my eyes.

Cinderella shall go to the ball, I think.

After an evening dinner and dancing with Big Daddy, I snuggle up to him, playfully rubbing my hand over his belly, drawing imaginary circles and tickling him. I am being careful not to bring him to arousal. 'Big Daddy', I say in my cutest voice, 'your baby has to travel and needs a passport'.

'Baaaby, no problem. What my baby wants, my baby will get. Big Daddy will sort it out for you. Just give me your details'.

I focus now on exams with no distractions. What better excuse to get rid of Dr Kunle? His 'I want to marry you' makes me just want to puke.

Within two weeks, I get a visit from Bulldog. He hands me a brown envelope. Excited, I tear it open. More dollars and a passport! My own brand-new Nigerian green passport.

The long wait for the exam results to be released means long, boring evenings. I don't really feel like partying as the other girls have been doing since the end of exams, nor do I feel like dancing for Big Daddy. Come to think of it, I have not seen or heard from him since Bulldog delivered my passport. This leaves me with not much choice but to hang with Dr Kunle over the weekend at the jazz bar, which is getting rather boring now. He now refuses to take me to the Shrine. No good girl should be seen there, he says.

At last the results are released, and true to form, I have not disappointed myself. With my results in hand, and my required documents—passport and passbook—I join masses of people applying for visas at the British High Commission.

'Number eighty-three'. My number is called, and I present my application to the interviewer. He looks through my papers, takes a look at me, and says, 'So you have won a scholarship, Miss Pearce'.

'That's correct', I answer, failing to be intimidated by his interrogation.

'And when you complete your course, will you be returning to Nigeria?'

'Right now, I do not know', I reply.

He mumbles something under his breath. 'Take a seat outside and wait to be called'.

'Thank you'.

The wait is long, and I have mixed feelings, I look at the faces of dejected applicants whose applications have been declined and hear a tale of woe about how someone's father sold the family inheritance of land and property to raise funds to meet the criteria for the visa application. I refuse to let all that negativity pull me down.

'Miss Tolani Pearce'. I am handed my documents. London, here I come!

I do not wait for the graduation ceremony. There is no one to attend or to celebrate with. I say no good-byes to Big Daddy, no goodbyes to Dr Kunle. I leave the shores of Nigeria.

CHAPTER SEVENTEEN

The blast of cold wind hits my face as I disembark from the plane. The thin jumper I have on is not doing a very good job of keeping out the chill of the autumn wind. I marvel at how things are done in an orderly manner here in London. Queues for everything, even queues waiting for the buses—how interesting. I try to blend in as much as I can, so I try to avoid sitting next to old ladies on the buses. They tend to ask, 'How are you coping with the cold? Bet it's much colder than Africa, innit?'

I soon make friends at the student accommodation with some girls from Kenya who are also on scholarship. We share jokes about not having chili in our chili con carne and how we have to put on several layers to keep warm, even though it's only early September.

I start the academic year with a year-long internship at the palliative care unit at the Royal Free Hospital. I care for the patients who are at the end of life's journey. Some have relatives who visit, but a lot do not have visitors at all. I find it most rewarding to sit there reading to them passages from the selection of books at the little library or just sitting with them, holding their hands as they slowly pass on.

As usual, during my quiet evening, just before the end of my shift, I sit to read from a passage of William Shakespeare's poem 'All the World's a Stage' to an elderly man who appears to have a reason to keep hanging on every day.

'Ahem, ahem'. I hear someone clearing his throat and look up to see who has come to visit. I nearly drop the book and almost knock over the jug of water and flowers on the side table. Jeff! Jeff Norfolk! I rush to give him a hug, forgetting where I am for a moment.

'Jeff Norfolk! I cannot believe my eyes'.

'Hello T'lani, I have watched you look after my grandfather and read to him every evening '

'thank you for looking after Mr Norfolk senior'. And then I hear the old man take his last breath.

After the end of my shift, I meet up with Jeff at the coffee shop down the road, and do we have a lot of catching up!

'T'lani, what happened to you?'

'It's a long story, Jeff. It's a veerry long story. But tell me, how did you just leave suddenly?'

'Well, what I thought would be a few months turned to be years', Jeff says. 'I went back to Lagos regularly in the hope that you would turn up but had nowhere to look for you. So I gave up and returned finally to the UK. I met Lorna, a Green Peace activist. She was part of a group demonstrating outside our head office. We got to chatting, went on a few dates, and kind of fell in love'.

'How bizarre!' I say.

'Yes! And what's even more bizarre, we got married and went to Kenya for our honeymoon. On the last day, we were due to return to London, but Lorna was nowhere to be found. She left me a note saying that she had fallen in love with the tour guide, a Massai warrior, and had gone to live with him. So I return to the UK without a wife, single and just got on with things, including visiting my grandfather in hospital.

I try to hold myself back from laughing and pretend to be sad for him.

We walk down Primrose Hill hand in hand, disturbing the fallen leaves of autumn in our path. Slowly Jeff turns me around to face him, and we lock in a warm embrace.

'Thank you, T'lani, for keeping a place for me in your heart'.

'Thank you, Jeff Norfolk, for being at the end of my rainbow'.

Printed in Great Britain
by Amazon.co.uk, Ltd.,
Marston Gate.